I0764416

AN ARKANSAS PLANTER

OPIE READ

An Arkansas Planter

Opie Read

PO Box 2211
Fairfield, IA 52556
www.1stworldlibrary.com
First Edition

LCCN: 2007935405

Softcover ISBN: 978-1-4218-9357-0
Hardcover ISBN: 978-1-4218-9457-7
eBook ISBN: 978-1-4218-9257-3

1st World Library Literary Society

Giving Back to the World

"If you want to work on the core problem, it's early school literacy."

- James Barksdale, former CEO of Netscape

"No skill is more crucial to the future of a child, or to a democratic and prosperous society, than literacy."

- Los Angeles Times

"Literacy... means far more than learning how to read and write... The aim is to transmit... knowledge and promote social participation."

- UNESCO

"Literacy is not a luxury, it is a right and a responsibility. If our world is to meet the challenges of the twenty-first century we must harness the energy and creativity of all our citizens."

- President Bill Clinton

"Parents should be encouraged to read to their children, and teachers should be equipped with all available techniques for teaching literacy, so the varying needs and capacities of individual kids can be taken into account."

- Hugh Mackay

CHAPTER I

Lying along the Arkansas River, a few miles below Little Rock, there is a broad strip of country that was once the domain of a lordly race of men. They were not lordly in the sense of conquest; no rusting armor hung upon their walls; no ancient blood-stains blotched their stairways—there were no skeletons in dungeons deep beneath the banquet hall. But in their own opinion they were just as great as if they had possessed these gracious marks of medieval distinction. Their country was comparatively new, but their fathers came mostly from Virginia and their whisky came wholly from Kentucky. Their cotton brought a high price in the Liverpool market, their daughters were celebrated for beauty, and their sons could hold their own with the poker players that traveled up and down the Mississippi River. The slave trade had been abolished, and, therefore, what remained of slavery was right; and in proof of it the pulpit contributed its argument. Negro preachers with wives scattered throughout the community urged their fellow bondsmen to drop upon their knees and thank God for the privilege of following a mule in a Christian land. The merciless work of driving the negroes to their tasks was performed by men from the North. Many a son of New England, who, with emotion, had listened to Phillips and to Garrison, had afterward hired his harsh energies to the slave owner. And it was this hard driving that taught the negro vaguely to despise the abolitionist. But as a class the slaves were not unhappy. They were ignorant, but the happiest song is sometimes sung by ignorance. They believed the Bible as read to them by the preachers, and the Bible told them that God had made them slaves; so, at evening, they twanged rude strings and danced the "buck" under the boughs of the cottonwood tree.

On the vine-shaded veranda the typical old planter was wont to sit, looking up and down the road, watching for a friend or a stranger—any one worthy to drink a gentleman's liquor, sir. His library was stocked with romances. He knew English history as handed down to him by the sentimentalist. He hated the name of king, but revered an aristocracy. No business was transacted under his roof; the affairs of his estate were administered in a small office, situated at the corner of the yard. His wife and daughters, arrayed in imported finery, drove about in a carriage. New Orleans was his social center, and he had been known to pay as much as a thousand dollars for a family ticket to a ball at the St. Charles hotel. His hospitality was known everywhere. He was slow to anger, except when his honor was touched upon, and then he demanded an apology or forced a fight. He was humorous, and yet the consciousness of his own dignity often restrained his enjoyment of the ludicrous. When the cotton was in bloom his possessions were beautiful. On a knoll he could stand and imagine that the world was a sea of purple.

That was the Arkansas planter years ago, before the great sentimental storm swept down upon him, before an evening's tea-table talk in Massachusetts became a tornado of iron in Virginia. When ragged and heart-sore he returned from the army, from as brave a fight as man ever engaged in, he sat down to dream over his vanished greatness. But his dream was short. He went to work, not to re-establish his former condition of ease—for that hope was beyond him—but to make a living for his family.

On a knoll overlooking the Arkansas River stood the Cranceford homestead. The site was settled in 1832, by Captain Luke Cranceford, who had distinguished himself in an Indian war. And here, not long afterward, was born John Cranceford, who years later won applause as commander of one of the most stubborn batteries of the Confederate Army. The house was originally built of cypress logs, but as time passed additions of boards and brick were made, resulting in a formless but comfortable habitation, with broad passage ways and odd lolling places set to entrap cool breezes. The plantation comprised about one thousand acres. The land for the most part was level, but here and there a hill arose, like a sudden jolt. From right to left the tract was divided by a bayou, slow and dark. The land was so valuable that most of it had been cleared years ago, but in the wooded stretches the timber was thick, and in places the tops of the trees were laced together with wild grape vines. Far away was a range of pine-covered hills, blue cones in the distance. And here lived the poorer class of people, farmers who could not hope to look to the production of cotton, but who for a mere existence raised thin hogs and nubbins of corn. In the lowlands the plantations were so large and the residences so far apart that the country would have appeared thinly settled but for the negro quarters here and there, log villages along the bayous.

In this neighborhood Major John Cranceford was the most prominent figure. The county was named in honor of his family. He was called a progressive man. He accepted the yoke of reconstruction and wore it with a laugh, until it pinched, and then he said nothing, except to tell his neighbors that a better time was coming. And it came. The years passed, and a man who had been prominent in the Confederate council became Attorney-General of the

American Nation, and men who had led desperate charges against the Federal forces made speeches in the old capitol at Washington. And thus the world was taught a lesson of forgiveness—of the true greatness of man.

In New Orleans the Major was known as a character, and his nerve was not merely a matter of conjecture. Courage is supposed to hold a solemn aspect, but the Major was the embodiment of heartiness. His laugh was catching; even the negroes had it, slow, loud and long. Sometimes at morning when a change of season had influenced him, he would slowly stride up and down the porch, seeming to shake with joviality as he walked. Years ago he had served as captain of a large steamboat, and this at times gave him an air of bluff authority. He was a successful river man, and was therefore noted for the vigor and newness of his profanity. His wife was deeply religious, and year after year she besought him to join the church, pleaded with him at evening when the two children were kissed good night—and at last he stood the rector's cross-examination and had his name placed upon the register. It was a hard struggle, but he weeded out his oaths until but one was left—a bold "by the blood." He said that he would part even with this safety valve but that it would require time; and it did. The Major believed in the gradual moral improvement of mankind, but he swore that the world intellectually was going to the devil. And for this conviction he had a graded proof. "Listen to me a minute," he was wont to say. "I'll make it clear to you. My grandfather was graduated with great honors from Harvard, my father was graduated with honor, I got through all right, but my son Tom failed."

CHAPTER II

One hot afternoon the Major sat in his library. The doors were open and a cool breeze, making the circuitous route of the passage ways, swept through the room, bulging a newspaper which he held opened out in front of him. He was scanning the headlines to catch the impulsive moods of the world. The parlor was not far away, down the hall, and voices reached him. And then there came the distressing hack, hack, of a hollow cough. He put down the newspaper, got up, and slowly strode about the room, not shaking with joviality as he walked. In the parlor the voices were hushed, there was a long silence, and then came the hollow cough. He sat down and again took up the newspaper, but the cough, hack, hack, smote him like the recurrence of a distressing thought, and he crumpled the paper and threw it upon the floor. Out in the yard a negro woman was singing; far down the stream a steamboat whistled. And again came the hollow cough. There was another long silence, and then he heard light footsteps in the hall. A young woman halted at the door and stood looking at him. Her face was pale and appeared thin, so eager was her expression. She was slight and nervous.

"Well," he said. She smiled at him and said, "Well." Then she slowly entered the room, and with a sigh took a seat near him. The cough from the parlor was more distressful, and she looked at him, and in her eyes was a beseeching sadness.

"Louise."

"Yes, sir."

"What did I tell you?"

"I don't know, sir."

"Don't say that, for you do know."

"You've told me so many things—"

"Yes, I know. But what did I tell you about Carl Pennington?"

"I don't know, sir."

"Yes you do. I told you that I didn't want him to come here. Didn't I?"

"Yes, sir."

"Then why is he here?"

"I met him and invited him to come."

"Ah, ha. But I don't want him here; don't want you to see him."

She sat looking at him as if she would study every line of his face. He shoved his hands deep into his pockets and looked down. The cough came again, and he looked at the girl. "You know the reason I don't want you to see him. Don't you?"

"Yes, sir, and I know the reason why I do want to see him."

"The devil—pardon me," he quickly added, withdrawing his hands from his pockets and bowing to her. She slightly inclined her head and smiled sadly. He looked hard at her, striving to read her thoughts; and she was so frail, her face was so thin and her eyes so wistful that she smote him with pity. He reached over and took one of her hands, and affectionately she gave him the other one. She tried to laugh. The cough came again, and she took her hands away. He reached for them, but she put them behind her. "No, not until I have told you," she said, and he saw her lip tremble. "He was afraid to come in here to see you," she went on, speaking with timid slowness. "He is so weak and sick that he can't stand to be scolded, so I have come to—" She hesitated. He shoved himself back and looked hard at her, and his eyebrows stuck out fiercely.

"To ask me what?" His voice was dry and rasping. "What can you ask me? To let him come here to see you? No, daughter. I can't permit that. And I don't intend to be cruel when I say this. I am sorry for him, God knows I deeply sympathize with him, but he must not hope to—"

"I was not going to ask you to let him come," she broke in. "I am going to ask you to let me go—go with him."

"By the blood!" the Major exclaimed, jumping to his feet. "What do you mean? Marry him?"

"Yes, sir," she quietly answered. He looked at her, frowning, his face puffed, his brows jagged. And then appearing to master himself he sat down and strove to take her hand, but she held it behind her. "My daughter, I want to talk to you, not in anger, but with common sense. It actually horrifies me to think of your marriage—I can't do it, that's all. Why, the poor fellow can't live three months; he is dead on his feet now. Listen at that cough. Louise, how can you think of marrying him? Haven't you any judgment at all? Is it possible that you have lost—but I won't scold you; I must reason with you. There is time enough for you to marry, and the sympathetic fancy that you have for that poor fellow will soon pass away. It must. You've got plenty of chances. Jim Taylor—"

"Why do you speak of him, father?"

"I speak of him because he loves you—because he is as fine a young fellow as walks the face of the earth."

"But, father, he is so big and strong that he doesn't need any one to love him."

At this the Major appeared not to know whether to laugh or to frown. But he did neither; he sat for a time with his hands on his knees, looking wonderingly, almost stupidly at her; and then he said: "Nonsense. Where did you pick up that preposterous idea? So strong that he doesn't need love! Why, strength demands love, and to a big man the love of a little woman—" She drew back from him as he leaned toward her and he did not complete the sentence. Her impatience made him frown. "Won't you let me reason with you?" he asked. "Won't you help me to suppress all appearance of displeasure?"

"It is of no use," she replied.

"What is of no use? Reason?"

"Argument."

"What! Do you mean—"

"I mean that I am going to marry him."

In her eyes there was no appeal, no pleading, for the look that she gave him was hard and determined. Harsh words flew to the Major's mind, and he shook with the repression of them; but he was silent. He shoved his hands into his pockets and she heard his keys rattling. He arose with a deep sigh, and now, with his hands behind him, walked up and down the room. Suddenly he faced about and stood looking down upon her, at the rose in her hair.

"Louise, one night on a steamboat there was a rollicking dance. It was a moonlight excursion. There was a splash and a cry that a woman had fallen overboard. I leaped into the river, grasped her, held her head above the stream, fighting the current. A boat was put out and we were taken on board, and then by the light of a lantern I found that I had saved the life of my own daughter. So, upon you, I have more than a father's claim—the claim of gallantry, and this you cannot disregard, and upon it I base my plea."

She looked up straight at him; her lips were half open, but she said nothing.

"You don't seem to understand," he added, seeming to stiffen his shoulders in resentment at the calmness with which she regarded him. "I tell you that I waive the authority of a father and appeal to your gratitude; I remind you that I saved your life—leaped into the cold water and seized you, not knowing whose life I was striving to save at the risk of losing my own. Isn't that worth some sort of return? Isn't it worth even the sacrifice of a whim? Louise, don't look at me that way. Is it possible that you don't grasp—" He hesitated and turned his face toward the parlor whence came again the cough, hollow and distressing. The sound died away, echoing down the hall, and a hen clucked on the porch and a passage door slammed.

"Louise," he said, looking at her.

"Yes, sir."

"Do you catch—"

"I catch everything, father. It was noble of you to jump into the river when you didn't know but that you might be drowned, and recognizing that you risked your life, and feeling a deep gratitude, it is hard to repay you with disobedience. Wait a moment, please. You must listen to me. It is hard to repay you with disobedience, but it cannot be helped. You say that Mr. Pennington is dying and I know that you speak the truth. He knows that he is dying, and he appeals to me not to let him die alone—not alone in words," she quickly added, "but with something stronger than words, his helplessness, his despair. Other people have appeared to shun him because he is dying, but—"

"Hold on," he broke in. "I deny that. No one has shunned him because he is dying. Everybody is sorry for him, and you know that I would do anything for him."

"Would you? Then let him die under this roof as my husband. Oh, look how poor and thin he is, so helpless, and dying day by day, with no relatives near him, with nothing in prospect but long nights of suffering. Please don't tell me that I shan't take care of him, for I feel that it is the strongest duty that will ever come to me. Listen how he coughs. Doesn't it appeal to you? How can you refuse—how can you remind me of the gratitude I owe you?"

Tears were streaming down her face. He bent over her, placed his hands upon her cheeks and kissed her, but instantly he drew back with his resentful stiffening of the shoulders.

"Louise, it can't be. No argument and no appeal can bring it about. It makes me shudder to think of it. Really I can't understand it. The situation to me is most unnatural. But I won't be harsh with you. But I must say that I don't know where you get your stubbornness. No, I won't be harsh. Let me tell you what I will agree to do. He may come to this house and stay here until—may stay here and the best of care shall be taken of him, and you may nurse him, but you must not bear his name. Will you agree to this?"

She shook her head. She had wiped away her tears and her eyes were strong and determined. "After conceding so much I don't see why you should refuse the vital point," she said.

"I can tell you why, and I am afraid that I must."

"Don't be afraid; simply tell me."

"But, daughter, it would seem cruel."

"Not if I demand it."

"Then you do demand it? Well, you shall know. His father served a term in the Louisiana penitentiary for forgery. And now you may ask why I ever let him come into this house. I will tell you. He had been teaching school here some time and I said nothing. One day during a rainstorm he stopped at the gate. He was sick and I invited him to come in. After that I could not find enough firmness to tell him not to come, he was so pale and weak. I see now that it was a false sympathy. Do you understand me? His father was a convict."

"Yes, I understand. He told me."

"By the blood on the Cross! Do you mean to say—Louise," he broke off, gazing upon her, "your mind is unsettled. Yes, you are crazy, and, of course, all your self-respect is gone. You needn't say a word, you are crazy. You are—I don't know what you are, but I know what I am, and now, after the uselessness of my appeal to your gratitude, I will assert the authority of a father. You shall not marry him."

"And would you kill a dying man?" she quietly asked.

The question jolted him, and he shouted out: "What do you mean by such nonsense? You know I wouldn't."

"Then I will marry him."

For a moment the Major's anger choked him. With many a dry rasp he strove to speak, and just as he had made smoother a channel for his words, he heard the hollow cough drawing nearer. He motioned toward a door that opened in an opposite direction, and the girl, after hesitating a moment, quickly stepped out upon a veranda that overlooked the river. The Major turned his eyes toward the other door, and there Pennington stood with a handkerchief tightly pressed to his mouth. For a time they were silent, one strong and severe, the other tremulous and almost spectral in the softened light.

"There is a chair, sir," said the Major, pointing.

"I thank you, sir; I don't care to sit down. I—I am very sorry that you are compelled to look upon me as—as you do, sir. And it is all my fault, I assure you, and I can't defend myself."

He dropped his handkerchief and looked down as if he were afraid to stoop to pick it up. The Major stepped forward, caught up the handkerchief, handed it to him and stepped back.

"Thank you, sir," Pennington said, bowing, and then, after a short pause, he added: "I don't know what to say in explanation of—of myself. But I should think, sir, that the strength of a man's love is a sufficient defense of any weakness he may possess—I mean a sufficient defense of any indiscretion that his love has led him to commit. This situation stole upon me, and I was scarcely aware of its coming until it was here. I didn't know how serious—" He coughed his words, and when he became calmer, repeated his plea that love ought to excuse any weakness in man. "Your daughter is an angel of mercy," he said. "When I found myself dying as young as I was and as hopeful as I had been my soul filled up with a bitter resentment against nature and God, but she drew out the bitterness and instilled a sweetness and a prayer. And now to take her from me would be to snatch away the prospect of that peaceful life that lies beyond the grave. Sir, I heard you tell her that she was crazy. If so, then may God bless all such insanity."

He pressed the handkerchief to his mouth, racking, struggling; and when the convulsive agony had passed he smiled, and there in the shadow by the door the light that crossed his face was ghastly, like a dim smear of phosphorus. And now the Major's shoulders were not stiffened with resentment; they were drooping with a pity that he could not conceal, but his face was hard set, the expression of the mercy of one man for another, but also the determination to protect a daughter and the good name of an honored household.

"Mr. Pennington, I was never so sorry for any human being as I am for you at this moment, but, sir, the real blessings of this life come through justice and not through impulsive mercy. In thoughtless sympathy a great wrong may lie, and out of a marriage with disease may arise a generation of misery. We are largely responsible for the ailments of those who are to follow us. The wise man looks to the future; the weak man hugs the present. You say that my daughter is an angel of mercy. She has ever been a sort of sister of charity. I confess that I have never been able wholly to understand her. At times she has even puzzled her mother, and a daughter is odd, indeed, when a mother cannot comprehend her. I am striving to be gentle with you, but I must tell you that you cannot marry her. I don't want to tell you to go, and yet it is better that this interview should come to a close."

He bowed to Pennington and turned toward the veranda that overlooked the river, but a supplicating voice called him back. "I wish to say," said the consumptive, "that from your point of view you are right. But that does not alter my position. You speak of the misery that arises from a marriage with disease. That was very well put, but let me say, sir, that I believe that I am growing stronger. Sometimes I have thought that I had consumption, but in my saner moments I know that I have not. I can see an improvement from day to day. Several days ago I couldn't help coughing, but now at times I can suppress it. I am growing stronger."

"Sir," exclaimed the Major, "if you were as strong as a lion you should not marry her. Good day."

CHAPTER III

Slowly and heavily the Major walked out upon the veranda. He stood upon the steps leading down into the yard, and he saw Louise afar off standing upon the river's yellow edge. She had thrown her hat upon the sand, and she stood with her hands clasped upon her brown head. A wind blew down the stream, and the water lapped at her feet. The Major looked back into the library, at the door wherein Pennington had stood, and sighed with relief upon finding that he was gone. He looked back toward the river. The girl was walking along the shore, meditatively swinging her hat. He stepped to the corner of the house, and, gazing down the road, saw Pennington on a horse, now sitting straight, now bending low over the horn of the saddle. The old gentleman had a habit of making a sideward motion with his hand as if he would put all unpleasant thoughts behind him, and now he made the motion not only once, but many times. And it seemed that his thoughts would not obey him, for he became more imperative in his pantomimic demand.

At one corner of the large yard, where the smooth ground broke off into a steep slope to the river, there stood a small office built of brick. It was the Major's executive chamber, and thither he directed his steps. Inside this place his laugh was never heard; at the door his smile always faded. In this commercial sanctuary were enforced the exactions that made the plantation thrive. Outside, in the yard, in the "big house," elsewhere under the sky, a plea of distress might moisten his eyes and soften his heart to his own financial disadvantage, but under the moss-grown shingles of the office all was business, hard, uncompromising. It was told in the neighborhood that once, in this inquisition of affairs, he demanded the last cent possessed by a widowed woman, but that, while she was on her way home, he overtook her, graciously returned the money and magnanimously tore to pieces a mortgage that he held against her small estate.

Just as he entered the office there came across the yard a loud and impatient voice. "Here, Bill, confound you, come and take this horse. Don't you hear me, you idiot? You infernal niggers are getting to be so no-account that the last one of you ought to be driven off the place. Trot, confound you. Here, take this horse to the stable and feed him. Where is the Major? In the office? The devil he is."

Toward the office slowly strode old Gideon Batts, fanning himself with his white slouch hat. He was short, fat, and bald; he was bowlegged with a comical squat; his eyes stuck out like the eyes of a swamp frog; his nose was enormous, shapeless, and red. To the Major's family he traced the dimmest line of kinship. During twenty years he had operated a small plantation that belonged to the Major, and he was always at least six years behind with his rent. He had married the widow Martin, and afterward swore that he had been disgracefully deceived by her, that he had expected much but had found her moneyless; and after this he had but small faith in woman. His wife died and he went into contented mourning, and out of gratitude to his satisfied melancholy, swore that he would pay his rent, but failed. Upon the Major he held a strong hold, and this was a puzzle to the neighbors. Their characters stood at fantastic and whimsical variance; one never in debt, the other never out of debt; one clamped by honor, the other feeling not its restraining pinch. But together they would ride abroad, laughing along the road. To Mrs. Cranceford old Gid was a pest. With the shrewd digs of a woman, the blood-letting side stabs of her sex, she had often shown her disapproval of the strong favor in which the Major held him; she vowed that her husband had gathered many an oath from Gid's swollen store of execration (when, in truth, Gid had been an apt pupil under the Major), and she had hoped that the Major's attachment to the church would of necessity free him from the humiliating association with the old sinner, but it did not, for they continued to ride abroad, laughing along the road.

Like a skittish horse old Gid shied at the office door. Once he had crossed that threshold and it had cost him a crop of cotton.

"How are you, John?" was Gid's salutation as he edged off, still fanning himself.

"How are you, sir?" was the Major's stiff recognition of the fact that Gid was on earth.

"Getting hotter, I believe, John."

"I presume it is, sir." The Major sat with his elbow resting on a desk, and about him were stacked threatening bundles of papers; and old Gid knew that in those commercial romances he himself was a familiar character.

"Are you busy, John?"

"Yes, but you may come in."

"No, I thank you. Don't believe I've got time."

"Then take time. I want to talk to you. Come in."

"No, not to-day, John. Fact is I'm not feeling very well. Head's all stopped up with a cold, and these summer colds are awful, I tell you. It was a summer cold that took my father off."

"How's your cotton in that low strip along the bayou?"

"Tolerable, John; tolerable."

"Come in. I want to talk to you about it."

"Don't believe I can stand the air in there, John. Head all stopped up. Don't believe I'm going to live very long."

"Nonsense. You are as strong as a buck."

"You may think so, John, but I'm not. I thought father was strong, too, but a summer cold got him. I am getting along in years, John, and I find that I have to take care of myself. But if you really want to talk to me about that piece of cotton, come out under the trees where it's cool."

The Major shoved back his papers and arose, but hesitated; and Gid stood looking on, fanning himself. The Major stepped out and Gid's face was split asunder with a broad smile.

"I gad. I've been up town and had a set-to with old Baucum and the rest of them. Pulled up fifty winner at poker and jumped. Devilish glad to see you; miss you every minute of the time I'm away. Let's go over there and sit down on that bench."

They walked toward a bench under a live-oak tree, and upon

Gid's shoulder the Major's hand affectionately rested. They halted to laugh, and old Gid shoved the Major away from him, then seized him and drew him back. They sat down, still laughing, but suddenly the Major became serious.

"Gid, I'm in trouble," he said.

"Nonsense, my boy, there is no such thing as trouble. Throw it off. Look at me. I've had enough of what the world calls trouble to kill a dozen ordinary men, but just look at me—getting stronger every day. Throw it off. What is it, anyway?"

"Louise declares that she is going to marry Pennington!"

"What!" old Gid exclaimed, turning with a bouncing flounce and looking straight at the Major. "Marry Pennington! Why, she shan't, John. That's all there is of it. We object and that settles it. Why, what the deuce can she be thinking about?"

"Thinking about him," the Major answered.

"Yes, but she must quit it. Why, it's outrageous for as sensible a girl as she is to think of marrying that fellow. You leave it to me; hear what I said? Leave it to me."

This suggested shift of responsibility did not remove the shadow of sadness that had fallen across the Major's countenance.

"You leave it to me and I'll give her a talk she'll not forget. I'll make her understand that she's a queen, and a woman is pretty devilish skittish about marrying anybody when you convince her that she's a queen. What does your wife say about it?"

"She hasn't said anything. She's out visiting and I haven't seen her since Louise told me of her determination to marry him."

"Don't say determination, John. Say foolish notion. But it's all right."

"No, it's not all right."

"What, have you failed to trust me? Is it possible that you have lost faith in me? Don't do that, John, for if you do it will be a never failing source of regret. You don't seem to remember what my powers of persuasion have accomplished in the past. When I was in the legislature, chairman of the Committee on County and County Lines, what did my protest do? It kept them from cutting off a ten-foot strip of this county and adding it to Jefferson. You must remember those things, John, for in the factors of persuasion lie the shaping of human life. I've been riding in the hot sun and I think that a mint julep would hit me now just about where I live. Say, there, Bill, bring us some mint, sugar and whisky. And cold water, mind you. Oh, everything will come out all right. By the way, do you remember that Catholic priest that came here with a letter of introduction to you?"

"Yes, his name is Brennon."

"Yes, that's it. But how did he happen to bring a letter to you?"

"He came from Maryland with a letter given him by a relative of mine."

"Yes, and he has gone to work, I tell you. Do you know what he's doing? Reaching out quietly and gathering the negroes into his church. And there are some pretty wise men behind him. They didn't send an Irishman or a Dutchman or an Italian, but an American from an old family. He's already got three negroes on my place, and Perdue tells me that he's nipping one now and then over his way. There's a scheme in it, John."

"There is a scheme in all human affairs, and consequently in all church movements," the Major replied, and the impulse of a disquisition straightened him into a posture more dignified, for he was fond of talking and at times he strove to be logical and impressive; but at this moment Bill arrived with mint from the spring; and with lighter talk two juleps were made.

"Ah," said old Gideon, sipping his scented drink, "virtue may become wearisome, and we may gape during the most fervent prayer, but I gad, John, there is always the freshness of youth in a mint julep. Pour just a few more drops of liquor into mine, if you please—want it to rassle me a trifle, you know. Recollect those come-all ye songs we used to sing, going down the river? Remember the time I snatched the sword out of my cane and lunged at a horse trader from Tennessee? Scoundrel grabbed it and broke it off and it was all I could do to keep him from establishing a close and intimate relationship with me. Great old days, John; and I Gad, they'll never come again."

"I remember it all, Gid, and it was along there that you fell in love with a woman that lived at Mortimer's Bend."

"Easy, now, John. A trifle more liquor, if you please. Thank you. Yes, I used to call her the wild plum. Sweet thing, and I had no idea that she was married until her lout of a husband came down to the landing with a double-barrel gun. Ah, Lord, if she had been single and worth money I could have made her very happy. Fate hasn't always been my friend, John."

"Possibly not, Gid, but you know that fate to be just should divide her favors, and this time she leaned toward the woman."

"Slow, John. I Gad, there's your wife."

A carriage drew up at the yard gate and a woman stepped out. She did not go into the house, but seeing the Major, came toward him. She was tall, with large black eyes and very gray hair. In her step was suggested the pride of an old Kentucky family, belles, judges and generals. She smiled at the Major and bowed stiffly at old Gid. The two men arose.

"Thank you, I don't care to sit down," she said. "Where is Louise?"

"I saw her down by the river just now," the Major answered.

"I wish to see her at once," said his wife.

"Shall I go and call her, madam?" Gid asked.

She gave him a look of surprise and answered: "No, I thank you."

"No trouble, I assure you," Gid persisted. "I am pleased to say that age has not affected my voice, except to mellow it with more of reverence when I address the wife of a noble man and the mother of a charming girl."

She had dignity, but humor was never lost upon her, and she smiled. This was encouraging and old Gid proceeded: "I was just telling the Major of my splendid prospects for a bountiful crop this year, and I feel that with this blessing of Providence I shall soon be able to meet all my obligations. I saw our rector, Mr. Mills, this morning, and he spoke of how thankful I ought to be—he had just passed my bayou field—and I told him that I would not only assert my gratitude but would prove it with a substantial donation to the church at the end of the season."

In the glance which she gave him there was refined and gentle contempt; and then she looked down upon the decanter of whisky. Old Gideon drew down the corners of his mouth, as was his wont when he strove to excite compassion.

"Yes," he said with a note of pity forced upon his voice, "I am exceedingly thankful for all the blessings that have come to me, but I haven't been very well of late, rather feeble to-day, and the kind Major, noticing it, insisted upon my taking a little liquor, the medicine of our sturdy and gallant fathers, madam."

The Major sprawled himself back with a roaring laugh, and hereupon Gid added: "It takes the Major a long time to get over a joke. Told him one just now and it tickled him mighty nigh to death. Well, I must be going now, and, madam, if I should chance to see anything of your charming daughter, I will tell her that you desire a conference with her. William," he called, "my horse, if you please."

CHAPTER IV

Mrs. Cranceford had met Pennington in the road, and on his horse, in the shade of a cottonwood tree, he had leaned against the carriage window to tell her of his interview with the Major. He had desperately appealed to the sympathy which one with so gentle a nature must feel for a dying man, and had implored her to intercede with her husband; but with compassionate firmness she had told him that no persuasion could move her husband from the only natural position he could take, and that she herself was forced to oppose the marriage.

The Major, with his hands behind him, was now walking up and down the short stretch of shade. "I don't wonder that the absurdity of it does not strike him," he said, "for he is a drowning sentimentalist, catching at a fantastic straw." He paused in his walk to look at his wife as if he expected to find on her face a commendation of this simile. She nodded, knowing what to do, and the Major continued, resuming his walk: "I say that I can't blame him so much, but Louise ought to have better sense. I'll swear I don't know where she gets her stubbornness. Oh, but there is no use worrying ourselves with a discussion of it. You may talk to her, but I have had my say."

Louise, meanwhile, was strolling along a shaded lane that led from the ferry. Iron weeds grew in the corners of the fence, and in one hand she carried a bunch of purple blooms; with the other hand she slowly swung her hat, holding the strings. A flock of sheep came pattering down the road. With her hat she struck at the leader, a stubborn dictator demanding the whole of the highway. His flock scampered off in a fright, leaving him doggedly eyeing the disputer of his progress. But now she was frightened, with such fierceness did the old ram lower his head and gaze at her, and she cried out, "Go on back, you good-for-nothing thing."

"He won't hurt you," a voice cried in the woods, just beyond the fence. "Walk right up to him."

An enormous young fellow came up to the fence and with climbing over broke the top rail. "Don't you see he's scared?"

"But he would have knocked me over if you hadn't come."

"No, he wouldn't; he was just trying to make friends with you."

"But I don't want such a friend."

Together they slowly walked along. With tenderness in his eyes he looked down upon her, and when he spoke, which he did from time to time, his voice was deep and heavy but with a mellowness in it. She addressed him as Mr. Taylor and asked him if he had been away. And he said that he had, but that was not a sufficient reason for the formality of Mister—his name was Jim. She looked up at him—and her eyes were so blue that they looked black—and admitted that his name had been Jim but that now it must be Mr. Taylor. She laughed at this but his face was serious.

"Why, I haven't called you Jim since—"

"Since I asked you to marry me."

"No, not since then. And now you know it wouldn't be right to call you Jim."

In his slowness of speech he floundered about, treading down the briars that grew along the edge of the road, walking with heavy tread but tenderly looking down upon her. "That ought not to make any difference," he said. "I knew you before you—before you knew anything, and now it doesn't sound right to hear you call me anything but Jim. It is true that the last time I saw you—seems a long time, but it wasn't more than a week ago—you said that you wouldn't marry me, and really the time seems so long that I didn't know but you might have changed your mind."

"No, not yet," she replied.

"But you might."

"No, I couldn't."

"Is it as bad as that?"

"It's worse; it would be impossible for me to change."

"I don't suppose you know why?"

"Yes, I do. I am going to be married."

"What!" He stopped, expecting her to obey his own prompting and halt also, but she walked on. With long strides he overtook her, passed her, stood in front of her. She stepped aside and passed on. But again he overtook her, but this time he did not seek to detain her.

"I can't believe it," he said, stripping the leaves from the thorn bushes and briars that came within touch of his swinging hand. "I don't believe that you would marry a man unless you loved him and who—who—"

"Somebody," she said.

"Please don't tantalize me in this way. Tell me all about it."

"You know Mr. Pennington—"

"Who, that poor fellow!" he cried. "You surely don't think of marrying him. Louise, don't joke with me. Why, he can't live more than three months."

Now she halted and there was anger in her eyes as she looked at him, and resentful rebuke was in her voice when she spoke. "And you, too, fix the length of time he is to live. Why do you all agree to give him three months? Is that all the time you are willing to allow him?"

He stepped back from her and stood fumbling with his great hands. "I didn't know that any one else had given him three months," he replied. "I based my estimate merely on my recollection of how he looked the last time I saw him. I am willing to allow him all the time he wants and far more than Nature seems willing to grant."

"No, you are not. You all want him to die."

"Don't say that, Louise. You know that I ain't that mean. But I acknowledge that I don't want you to marry him."

"What need you care? If I refuse to marry you what difference does it make to you whom I marry?"

"It makes this difference—that I would rather see you the wife of a man that can take care of you. Louise, they say that I'm slow about everything, and I reckon I am, but when a slow man loves he loves for all time."

"I don't believe it; don't believe that any man loves for all time."

"Louise, to hear you talk one might think that you have been grossly deceived, but I know you haven't, and that is what forces me to say that I don't understand you."

"You don't have to understand me. Nobody has asked you to."

She walked on and he strode beside her, stripping the leaves off the shrubs, looking down at her, worshipping her; and she, frail and whimsical, received with unconcern the giant's adoration.

"I told the Major that I loved you—"

"Told him before you did me, didn't you?" she broke in, glancing up at him.

"No, but on the same day. I knew he was my friend, and I didn't know but—"

"That he would order me to marry you?"

"No, not that, but I thought he might reason with you."

"That's just like a stupid man. He thinks that he can win a woman with reason."

He pondered a long time, seeming to feel that this bit of

observation merited well-considered reply, and at last he said: "No, I didn't think that a woman could be won by something she didn't understand."

"Oh, you didn't. That was brilliant of you. But let us not spat with each other, Jim."

"I couldn't spat with you, Louise; I think too much of you for that, and I want to say right now that no matter if you do marry I'm going to keep on loving you just the same. I have loved you so long now that I don't know how to quit. People say that I am industrious, and they compliment me for keeping up my place so well, and for not going to town and loafing about of a Sunday and at night, but the truth is there ain't a dog in this county that's lazier than I am. During all these years my mind has been on you so strong that I have been driven to work."

She had thrown down her iron weed blossoms and had put her hands to her ears to shut out his words as if they were a reproach to her, but she heard him and thus replied: "It appears that I have been of some service at any rate."

"Yes, but now you are going to undo it all."

"I thought you said you were going to keep on loving me just the same."

"What! Do you want me to?" There was eagerness in his voice, and with hope tingling in his blood he remembered that a few moments before she had called him Jim. "Do you want me to?"

"I want you always to be my friend."

Under these words he drooped and there was no eagerness in

his voice when he replied: "Friendship between a great big man and a little bit of a woman is nonsense. They must love or be nothing to each other."

They had now reached the road that led past the Major's house. She turned toward home. "Wait a moment," he said, halting. She stopped and looked back at him. "Did you hear what I said?"

"What about?"

"Hear what I said about a big man and a little woman?"

"No, what did you say?"

He fumbled with his hands and replied: "No matter what I said then. What I say now is good-bye."

"Good-bye."

She tripped along as if she were glad to be rid of him, but after a time she walked slower as if she were deeply musing. She heard the brisk trotting of a horse, and, looking up, recognized Gideon Batts, jogging toward her. He saw her, and, halting in the shade, he waited for her to come up, and as she drew near he cried out, "Helloa, young rabbit."

She wrinkled her Greek nose at him, but she liked his banter, and with assumed offense she replied: "Frog."

"None of that, my lady."

"Well, then, what made you call me a young rabbit?"

"Because your ears stick out."

"I don't care if they do."

"Neither does a young rabbit."

"I call you a frog because your eyes stick out and because you are so puffy."

"Slow, now, my lady, queen of the sunk lands. Oh, but they are laying for you at home and you are going to catch it. I'd hate to be in your fix."

"And I wouldn't be in yours."

"Easy, now. You allude to my looks, eh? Why, I have broken more than one heart."

"Why, I didn't know you had been married but once."

He winced. "Look here, you mustn't talk that way."

"But you began it. You called me a young rabbit."

"That's right, and now we will call it off. What a memory you've got. I gad, once joke with a woman and her impudence—which she mistakes for wit—leaps over all difference in ages. But they are laying for you at home and you are going to catch it. I laughed at them; told them it was nonsense to suppose that the smartest girl in the state was going to marry—"

"You've said enough. I don't need your championship."

"But you've got it and can't help yourself. Why, so far as brains are concerned, the average legislator can't hold a candle to you."

"That's no compliment."

"Slow. I was in the legislature."

"Yes, one term, I hear."

"Why did you hear one term?"

"Because they didn't send you back, I suppose."

"Easy. But I tell you that the Major and your mother are furious. Your mother said—"

"She said very little in your presence."

"Careful. She said a great deal. But I infer from your insinuation that she doesn't think very well of me."

"You ought to know."

"I do; I know that she is wrong in her estimate of me. And I also know that I am right in my estimate of her. She is the soul of gentleness and quiet dignity. But you like me, don't you?"

"I am ashamed to say that I like you in spite of my judgment."

"Easy. That's good, I must say. Ah, the influence I have upon people is somewhat varied. Upon a certain type of woman, the dignified lady of a passing generation, I exercise no particular influence, but I catch the over-bright young women in spite of themselves. The reason you think so much of me is because you are the brightest young woman I ever saw. And this puts me at a loss to understand why you are determined to marry that fellow Pennington. Wait a moment.

I gad, if you go I'll ride along with you. Answer me one question: Is your love for him so great that you'll die if you don't marry him? Or is it that out of a perversity that you can't understand you are determined to throw away a life that could be made most useful? Louise, we have joked with each other ever since you were a child. In my waddling way I have romped with you, and I can scarcely realize that you are nearly twenty-four years old. Think of it, well advanced toward the age of discretion, and yet you are about to give yourself to a dying man. I don't know what to say."

"It seems not," she replied. And after a moment's pause she added: "If I am so well advanced toward the age of discretion I should be permitted to marry without the advice of an entire neighborhood."

She was now standing in the sun, looking up at him, her half-closed eyes glinting like blue-tempered steel.

"Is marriage wholly a matter of selfishness?" she asked.

"Slow. If you are putting that to me as a direct question I am, as a man who never shies at the truth, compelled to say that it is. But let me ask you if it is simply a matter of accommodation? If it is, why not send out a collection of handsome girls to marry an aggregation of cripples?"

Her eyes were wide open now and she was laughing. "No one could be serious with you, Mr. Gid."

"And no one could make you serious with yourself."

"Frog."

"Young rabbit."

She put her hands to her ears. "I would rather be a young rabbit than a frog."

"Wait a moment," he called as she turned away.

"Well."

"When you go home I wish you'd tell your mother that I talked to you seriously concerning the foolishness of your contemplated marriage. Will you do that much for your old playmate?"

She made a face at him and trippingly hastened away. He looked after her, shook his head, gathered up his bridle reins, and jogged off toward his home.

CHAPTER V

At home Louise made known her arrival by singing along the hallway that led to her room. She knew that not a very pleasant reception awaited her, and she was resolved to meet it with the appearance of careless gayety. She entered her room, drew back the curtains to admit the light, deftly touched her hair at the mirror, and sat down in a rocking chair. She took up a book, an American fad built upon a London failure, and was aimlessly turning the leaves when she heard her mother's voice.

"Are you in there, Louise?"

"Yes, come."

In the mother's appearance there was no suggestion of a stored rebuke; her gray hair, faultlessly parted, was smoothed upon her brow, her countenance bespoke calmness, and her sad eyes were full of tender love.

"Oh, you look so cool and sweet," said the girl. "Have this chair."

"No, thank you, I prefer to sit here."

She sat upon a straight-back chair. In her "day" only

grandmothers were supposed to sit in rockers; younger women were thought to preserve their health and their grace of form by sitting with rigid dignity upon chairs which might now be exhibited as relics of household barbarism.

"Did you have a pleasant visit?" the girl asked.

"Yes, very; but it was so warm over there under the hills that I was glad when the time came to leave."

"Does that Englishman still live alone on the Jasper place?"

"Yes, with his straight pipe and Scotch whisky. Perdue says that he appears to be perfectly contented there all alone."

"Have they found out anything about him?"

"No, only what he has been pleased to tell, and that isn't much. It seems that he is the younger son of a good family strayed off from home to better his condition."

"But why should he try to raise cotton when they say there is so little money in it, and especially when it requires experience? And the climate must be trying on him?"

"No, he says that the climate agrees with him. He has lived in India. He is reading American history and is much taken with the part the South has borne, so I learned from Mr. Perdue. He did not expect to find so little prejudice against foreigners. I could have told him that, in the South, an Englishman is scarcely looked upon as a foreigner—that is, among the best people."

They talked about many things that concerned them but little, of a new steamboat that had just entered upon the commerce of the lower river, of a cotton gin that was burned the night before, of the Catholic priest who had come to gather the negroes into his church; and surely they were far from a mention of Pennington. But suddenly Louise moved with uneasiness, for she had caught something that had not been said, that had not been looked, and, springing to her feet, she almost threw herself upon her mother, and with her arms about her, she cried: "Please don't say a word; please don't. I can argue with father, but I can't argue with you, for you take everything so to heart and suffer so much. Please don't speak anybody's name—don't say that father has said anything to you about anybody. You mustn't cry, either. Leave it all to me, and if I was born to wring your dear heart—there, let us hush."

She straightened up, putting the hair out of her eyes, and the silent and stately woman sat there with the tears rolling down her face. "Please don't, mother. You'll make me think I'm the meanest creature in the world. And I don't know but that I am, but I can't help it. Just call me unnatural, as you have done so many times, and let it all go. There, just listen at father walking up and down the porch; and I know he's mad at me."

"No, my child, he is not angry; he is hurt."

"Please don't say that. I don't want to hurt him. I would rather make him mad than to hurt him. Oh, I don't know what ails me, I am so restless and unhappy. I have tried every way to cure myself, but can't—I have read and read until I haven't any sense, and now I don't know what to do. But don't you tell me what not to do; don't say anything, but be your own sweet self."

She took up a brush from the dresser, touched her mother's hair, and said: "Let me, please." She loosened the thick coil. "Beautiful," she said. "Don't you know how I used to tease you to let me comb it, a long time ago? But it wasn't as pretty then as it is now."

Through her fingers the white hair streamed, glinting in the light now sobered by the falling of dusk.

The Major's step was heard at the door. "Come in, father. See, I am at my old employment." And in their faces and in the hair streaming through his daughter's fingers the old man read that all was well. He stood smiling at them. Out in the yard the fox-hounds began to yelp, and a galloping horse stopped with a loud, jolting "gluck" at the gate. Then came authoritative commands, and then a jar as if some one had leaped upon the porch. There was brisk walking, the opening and slamming of doors, and then at Louise's door a voice demanded: "What are you all doing here in the dark? Ain't supper ready? I'm as hungry as a she bear."

The Major's son Tom had arrived. And just at that moment, and before any one replied to him, the supper bell began to ring. "Takes me to bring things about, eh? You people might have waited here hungry for an hour. What are you doing here, anyway? Lou brushing mam's hair and pap looking on like a boy at a show."

"Thomas," said his mother, "I wish you wouldn't be so rough. There, daughter, that will do. Just coil it. That's it; thank you. Major, I do wish you wouldn't laugh at the brusqueness of your son; you encourage him."

Tom took his mother by the shoulders and turned her face toward the door. He was a clean-looking, blondish fellow, younger than his sister—an athlete, a boxer, with far more restlessness of muscle than absorption of mind. He had failed at Harvard, where his great-grandfather had distinguished himself; he had, with the influence of a Congressman, secured a West Point cadetship, and there had fallen under the rapid fire of a battery of mathematics, and had come home scouting at the humiliation which he had put upon his parents, and was now ready to submit himself to any other test that might present itself—was ready to borrow, to lend, or to fight. He picked negro tunes on a banjo, and had been heard hoarsely to sing a love song under a cypress tree. He had now just returned from the capital of the state, where he had spent two days watching the flank movements of a military drill.

"You people seem to be mighty solemn," was Tom's observation as they sat down to supper, glancing from one to another, and finally directing a questioning look at his father. "What's the trouble? What's happened? Is it possible that old Gideon has paid his rent?"

Louise laughed, a wrinkle crept across Mrs. Cranceford's brow and the Major sprawled back with a loud "haw." Gid's rent was a standing joke; and nothing is more sacredly entitled to instant recognition than a joke that for years has been established in a Southern household.

"I notice that he never goes into the Major's office," Mrs. Cranceford remarked; and Tom quickly replied: "And I don't blame him for that. I went in there about a month ago and haven't had a dollar since."

The Major did not laugh at this. The reputed exaction of his executive chamber was a sore spot to him. "How you robbers, young and old, would like to fleece me," he said. "And if I didn't turn to defensive stone once in a while you'd pull out my eye teeth."

"Don't see how anybody could get hold of your eye teeth, dad," Tom replied. "You are always busy cutting them when

I come round. Oh, by the way," he added with sudden seriousness, "you remember that fellow Mayo, the one that ran for County Clerk down here some time ago?"

"The scoundrel who swore he was elected?"

"That's the man. He disappeared, you know, after his trouble down here, then he went on from one community to another, a Democrat one season and a Republican the next, and now he has returned as a labor leader. I met him yesterday in Little Rock, and I never have seen a more insolent ruffian. He makes no secret of his plans, and he says that blood is bound to flow. I asked him if he had any to spare, and he cocked his eye at me and replied that he didn't know but he had."

The Major was silent, abstractedly balancing his knife on the rim of his plate. Mayo, an adventurer, a scoundrel with a brutish force that passed for frankness, had at one time almost brought about an uprising among the negroes of Cranceford County, and eager ears in the North, not the ears of the old soldier, but of the politician, shutting out the suggestions of justice, heard only the clamor of a political outrage; and again arose the loud cry that the South had robbed the inoffensive negro of his suffrage. But the story, once so full of alarm, was beginning to be a feeble reminiscence; Northern men with business interests in the South had begun to realize that the white man, though often in the wrong, could sometimes be in the right. But now a problem—graver than the over-thrashed straw of political rights, was about to be presented.

"I was in hopes that somebody had killed that fellow," said the Major, and his wife looked up with gentle reproof. "Don't say that, dear. The Lord will take him in His own good time."

The old gentleman winked at Tom. "I don't know about that," he replied. "I am afraid that the Lord in His management of the universe has forgotten him."

"John, please don't talk that way." When she was very serious she called him John. "When you speak so lightly you make me afraid that your relationship with the church is not very sacred to you."

"It's serious at any rate, Margaret."

"What do you mean by that, John?"

"Why," Tom cried, "it means that you dragged him into the pow-wow."

"Thomas"—and this time her reproof was not very gentle—"I won't stand that from you. And daughter," she added, speaking to Louise, "it is not a laughing matter. It all comes from so close an association with that good-for-nothing old Gideon. I know it does, and you needn't say a word. Nothing is sacred to him; he has no respect for God and cares nothing for man except to the extent that he can use him."

The Major strove to wink at Tom, but there was a hitch in his eye. "My dear, you don't understand the old fellow," said he. "And therefore you misjudge him. I know that he is weak, but I also know that he is strong, and he is quite as necessary to me as I am to him. He rests me, and rest is as essential as work. Sometimes the perfect gentleman is a bore; sometimes the perfect lady is tiresome. In man there is a sort of innocent evil, a liking for the half depraved and an occasional feeding of this appetite heightens his respect for the truly virtuous."

"I don't believe it, John."

"Of course you don't. You are the truly virtuous, and—" he spread himself back with a loud "haw," and sat there shaking under her cool gaze. "There, Margaret," he said, wiping his eyes, "don't take it to heart. I am doing the best I can and that is all the excuse I have to offer. I'm getting old; do you realize that? The things that used to amuse me are flat now and I can't afford to kill an amusement when one does happen to come along. Don't you worry about Gid. Why, Margaret, he has stood by me when other men turned their backs. The river was dangerous during my day, and the pop of a pistol was as natural as the bark of a dog. But old Gid was there by me."

"Oh, I don't doubt that he has some good qualities," she admitted. "But why doesn't he mend his ways?"

"Oh, he hasn't time for that, Margaret. He's too busy with other matters. There, now, we won't talk about him. But I promise you, my dear, that he shall not unduly influence me. I don't exactly know what I mean by that, either. I mean that you need have no fear of my permitting him to weaken my respect for the church. Yes, I think that's about what I mean. But the fact is he has never tried to do that. But what's the use of this talk. I can sum up the whole situation by reminding you that I am the master. There, now, don't sigh—don't look so worried."

"But, John, it grieves me to hear you say that you need him."

"Had to step back to pick that up, didn't you? Tom, after you're married you'll find that your wife will look with coldness or contempt upon your most intimate friend. It's the absurdest jealousy in woman's nature."

"Thomas," said his mother, "you will find nothing of the

sort; but I'll tell you what you may expect from the right sort of a wife—contempt for a coarse, low-bred fellow, should you insist upon holding him as your closest companion."

"Mother," Louise spoke up, "I think you are too severe. Mr. Batts is hemmed in with faults, but he has many good points. And I can understand why he is necessary to father. I am fond of him, and I am almost ready to declare that at times he is almost necessary to me. No, I won't make it as strong as that, but I must say that at times it is a keen pleasure to jower with him."

"To do what?" Mrs. Cranceford asked. "Jower with him? Where did you get that word?"

"It's one of his, picked up from among the negroes, I think, and it means more than dispute or wrangle. We jower at times—quarrel a little more than half in earnest."

"Well," said the mother, "perhaps I ought not to say anything, but I can't help it when I am so often hurt by that man's influence. Why, last Sunday afternoon your father left the rector sitting here and went away with that old sinner, and we heard them haw-hawing over in the woods. But I won't say any more."

"You never do, Margaret," the Major replied, winking at Louise. "But let us drop him. So you saw Mayo, eh?" he added, turning to Tom.

"Yes, sir, and I understand that he is coming back down here to prove to the negroes that we are cheating them out of their earnings."

The Major tossed a cigar to Tom, lighted one, and had begun to talk with a rhetorical and sententious balancing of periods—which, to his mind, full of the oratory of Prentiss, was the essence of impressiveness—when a negro woman entered the room. And hereupon he changed the subject.

When bedtime came the old gentleman stood on a rug in front of a large fire-place, meditatively winding his watch. His wife sat on a straight-back chair, glancing over the harmless advertisements in a religious newspaper. In the parlor they had spent an agreeable evening, with music and with never an allusion to an unpleasant subject, but there was something finer than an allusion, and it had passed from husband to wife and back again—a look at each other and a glance toward Louise. But they had laughed at the girl's imitation of a cakewalk, and yet in the minds of the father and the mother was the low echo of a hollow cough. Affectionately she had kissed them good night, and had started off down the hall in mimicry of a negro belle's walk, but they had heard her door shut with a quick slam as if she were at last impelled to be truthful with herself, to close herself in with her own meditations.

The Major hung his watch on a nail above the mantel-piece. From a far-off nook of the sprawling old house came the pling-plang of the boy's banjo.

"Margaret?"

"Yes, dear."

"What did you say to her?"

She began to fold the newspaper. "I didn't say anything. She wouldn't permit me."

"What do you think?"

"That she will do as she pleases."

"Consoling, by the—consoling, I must say. But I tell you she won't. I will shame her out of it."

CHAPTER VI

The top of the cotton stalk glimmered with a purple bloom, but down between the rows, among the dying leaves, the first bolls were opening. The air was still hot, for at noontime the glare in the sandy road was fierce, but the evening was cool, and from out in the gleaming dew came a sweetly, lonesome chirrup, an alarm in the grass, the picket of the insect army, crying the approach of frost. In the atmosphere was felt the influence of a reviving activity; new cotton pens were built along the borders of the fields, and the sounds of hammer and saw were heard in the neighborhood of the gin-house. With the dusk of Saturday evening "new" negroes came. In the city they had idled the summer away, gambling, and had now come with nimble fingers to pick cotton during the day and with tricky hands to throw dice at night. Gaunt, long-legged birds flew from the North and awkwardly capered on a sand-bar. Afar off there appeared to hover over the landscape a pall of thin, pale smoke; but, like the end of the rainbow, it stole back from closer view, was always afar off, lying low to the earth. The autumn rains had not yet set in, and the water in the bayou was low and yellow. The summer grapes were ripe, and in the cool, shaded coves at the base of the hills the muscadine was growing purple. The mules, so over-worked during plow-time, now stumbled down the lane, biting at one another. The stiffening wind, fore-whistle of the season's change of tune, was shrill amid the rushes at the edge of the swamp.

It was a time to work, but also to muse and dream while working. In the air was something that invited, almost demanded reverie. Upon the fields there might lie many a mortgage, but who at such a time could worry over the harsh exactions of debt?

Nearly three weeks had passed, and not again in the Major's household had Pennington's name been mentioned. But once, alone with his wife, the Major was leading up to it when she held up her hands and besought him to stop. "I can't bear to think of it," she said. "It stuns and stupefies me. But it is of no use to say anything to her. She is of age and she is headstrong."

There was a dry rasp in the Major's throat. "Don't you think that to say she is a crank would be hitting nearer the mark?"

"No, I don't," his wife answered. "She is not a crank. She is a remarkably bright woman."

"Yes, she shows it. When a man does a fool thing he is weak, off, as they say; but when a woman jumps out of the enclosure of common sense we must say that she is bright."

"I thought you were going to shame her out of it?"

"I will, but she hasn't given me a chance. But we'll let it go. I believe she has repented of her folly and is too much humiliated to make a confession."

His wife smiled sadly. "Don't you think so?" he asked.

"No, I don't."

"Well, I must say that you are very calm over the situation."

"Didn't I tell you that I was stunned and stupefied by it?"

"Yes, that's all right, and there's no use in worrying with it. Common sense says that when you can't help a thing the best plan is to let it go until a new phase is presented."

And so they ceased to discuss the subject, but like a heavy weight it lay upon them, and under it they may have sighed their worry, but they spoke it not. From Tom this sentimental flurry had remained securely hidden. Sometimes the grave tone of his father's words, overheard at night, and his mother's distressful air, during the day, struck him with a vague apprehension, but his mind was not keen enough to cut into the cause of what he might have supposed to be a trouble; and so, he gave it none of his time, so taken up with his banjo, his dogs, his sporting newspaper, and his own sly love affair. In Louise's manner no change was observed.

One afternoon the Major, old Gid, and an Englishman named Anthony Low were sitting on the porch overlooking the river when the Catholic priest from Maryland, Father Brennon, stopped to get a drink of water. And he was slowly making his way across the yard to the well when the Major called him, urging him to come upon the porch and rest himself. "Wait," the Major added, "and I'll have some water drawn for you."

"I thank you," the priest replied, bowing, "but I prefer to draw it." When he had drunk out of the bucket, he took a seat on the porch. He was a man of middle age, grave, and sturdy. His eyes were thoughtful and his smile was benevolent; his brow was high and broad, his nose large and strong, and a determined conviction seemed to have molded the shape of his mouth. His speech was slow, resonant, dignified; his accent of common words was Southern, but in some of his phrases was a slight burr, the subdued echo of a foreign tongue.

The Englishman was a stocky young fellow, with light hair and reddish side whiskers, a man of the world, doggedly careful in his use of superlatives, but with a habit of saying, "most extraordinary." He had rented an old plantation and lived alone in a dilapidated log house, with his briar pipe, Scotch whisky, sole leather hatbox, and tin bathtub. He had thought that it would be a sort of lark to grow a crop of cotton, and had hired three sets of negroes, discharging them in turn upon finding that they laughed at his ways and took advantage of his inexperience. He had made his first appearance by calling one morning at the Major's house and asking to be shown about the place. The Major gladly consented to do this, and together they set out on horseback.

The planter knew much of English hospitality, gathered from old romances, and now was come the time to show a Britain what an American gentleman could do. They rode down a lane, crossed a small field, and halted under a tree; and there was a negro with whisky, mint and sugar. They crossed a bayou, passed the "quarters," turned into the woods; and there was another negro with whisky, mint and sugar. They rode across a large field, and went through a gate, came to a spring; and there waiting for them was a negro with liquor for a julep. They turned into the "big" road, trotted along until they came to another spring, at least three miles from the starting point; and there was a negro with whisky, sugar and mint. But the Englishman's only comment was, "Ah, most extraordinary, how that fellow can keep ahead of us, you know."

Several months had elapsed, and the Major had called on Mr. Low, had shouted at the yard-gate, had supposed that no one was at home, had stalked into the wide open house and there had found the Englishman sitting in his bathtub, reading Huxley. And to-day Mr. Low had come to acknowledge the receipt of that visit.

"You are on the verge of your busy season," said the priest.

"Yes," the Major replied, "we begin picking to-morrow."

"A beautiful view across the whitening fields," said the priest.

"You ought to see my bayou field," old Gid spoke up. "It would make you open your eyes—best in the state. Don't you think so, John?"

"Well," the Major answered, "it is as good as any, I suppose."

"I tell you it's the best," Gid insisted. "And as a man of varied experience I ought to know what best is. Know all about cotton. I gad, I can look at a boll and make it open."

"Tell me," said the Englishman, "have you had any trouble with your labor?"

"With the negroes?" Gid asked. "Oh, no; they know what they've got to do and they do it. But let a cog slip and you can have all the trouble you want. I gad, you can't temporize with a negro. He's either your servant or your boss."

"All the trouble you want," said the Englishman. "By Jove, I don't want any. Your servant or your master. Quite remarkable."

"Don't know how remarkable it is, but it's a fact all the

same," Gid replied. "You've had trouble, I understand."

"Yes, quite a bit. I've had to drive them off a time or two; the rascals laughed at me. Quite full of fun they were, I assure you. I had thought that they were a solemn race. They are everywhere else except in America."

"It is singular," the Major spoke up, "but it is nevertheless true that the American negro is the only species of the African race that has a sense of humor. There's no humor in the Spanish negro, nor in the English negro, nor in fact in the American negro born north of the Ohio river, but the Southern negro is as full of drollery as a black bear."

"Ah, yes, a little too full of it, I fancy," Mr. Low replied. "I threatened them with the law, but they laughed the more and were really worse in every respect after that."

"With the law!" old Gid snorted. "What the deuce do they care about the law, and what sort of law do you reckon could keep a man from laughing? You ought to threatened them with a snake bone or a rabbit's foot."

"I beg pardon. A snake bone or a rabbit's foot, did you say? I really don't understand."

"Yes, threaten to conjure them. That might have fetched them."

"Ah, I see. Quite extraordinary, I assure you."

The priest began to talk, and with profound attention they turned to him. He sat there with the mystery of the medieval ages about him, with a great and silent authority behind him.

"Have you gentlemen ever considered the religious condition

of the negro? Have you not made his religion a joke? Is it not a popular belief that he will shout at his mourners' bench until midnight and steal a chicken before the dawn? He has been taught that religion is purely an emotion and not a matter of duty. He does not know that it means a life of inward humanity and outward obedience. I have come to teach him this, to save him; for in our church lies his only salvation, not alone of his soul, but of his body and of his rights as well as of his soul. I speak boldly, for I am an American, the descendant of American patriots. And I tell you that the Methodist negro and the Baptist negro and the Presbyterian negro are mere local issues; but the Catholic negro is international—he belongs to the great nervous system of Rome; and whenever Rome reaches out and draws him in, he is that moment removed as a turbulent element from politics. Although slavery was long ago abolished, there existed and to some small extent still exists a bond between the white man and the black man of the South—a sort of family tie; but this tie is straining and will soon be broken; a new generation is coming, and the negro and the white man will be two antagonistic forces, holding in common no sunny past—one remembering that his father was a master, the other that his father was a slave. When that time comes, and it is almost at hand, there will be a serious trouble growing out of a second readjustment. The Anglo-Saxon race cannot live on a perfect equality with any other race; it must rule; it demands complete obedience. And the negro will resent this demand, more and more as the old family ties are weakened. He has seen that his support at the North was merely a political sentiment, and must know that it will not sustain him in his efforts against capital, for capital, in the eye of capital, is always just, and labor, while unfortunate, is always wrong. And when the negro realizes this, remembering all his other wrongs, he will become desperate. That is the situation. But is there no way to avert this coming strife? I am here to say that there is. As communicants of the Catholic Church the negroes will not listen to the labor agitator. He will listen to the church, which will advise peace and submission to proper authority."

The priest had not gone far into his discourse before the Major began to walk up and down the porch in front of him, nodding at him each time as he passed. And when the clergyman ceased to speak, the Major, halting and facing him, thus replied: "There may be some truth, sir, in what you have said—there is some little truth in the wildest of speculation—but I should like to ask you why is not a Protestant negro in a Protestant country as safe as a Catholic negro in a Protestant country? You tell me that your religion will protect the negro, and I ask you why it does not protect the laborer in the North? You say that the Protestant negro in the South is a local issue, and I ask you why is not a Catholic laborer in the North an international issue? If the negro of the South, yielding to your persuasion, is to become a part of the great nervous system of Rome, why are not Catholic laborers everywhere a part of that system? I think, sir, that you have shrewdly introduced a special plea. Your church, with its business eyes always wide open, sees a chance to make converts and is taking advantage of it. And I will not say that I will oppose your cause. If the negro thinks that your church is better for him than the Protestant churches have proved themselves to be, why I say let him be taken in. I admit that we are not greatly concerned over the negro's religion. We are satisfied with the fact that he has his churches and that he has always been amply provided with preachers agreeing with him in creed and color of skin. I will concede that his professions of faith are regarded more or less in the light of a joke. But I want to tell you one thing—that the negro's best friends live here in the South. From us he knows exactly what to expect. He knows that he cannot rule us—knows that he must work for a living. The lands belong to the white man and the white man pays the taxes, and the white man would be a fool to permit the negro to manage his affairs. Men who dig in the coal mines of Pennsylvania don't manage the affairs of the company that owns the mines. I cannot question the correctness of one of your views—that the old tie is straining and may soon be broken. The old negroes still regard us with a sort of veneration, but if the younger ones show respect it is out of fear. Into this county a large number of negroes have lately come from Mississippi and South Carolina. They have been brought up on large plantations and have but a limited acquaintance with the white man. Instinctively they hate him. And these newcomers will listen to the voice of the agitator and by their example will lead their brethren into trouble. You are right when you say that the Anglo-Saxon race must rule. It will rule a community as it must eventually rule the civilized world. But I don't see how your church is to be the temporal as well as the spiritual salvation of the negro."

The Major sat down; the priest smiled gravely, showing the shape into which conviction and determination had molded his mouth. "My church is not at all times able to prevent labor troubles in the North," said he, "but it has often prevented the shedding of blood."

"Ah," the Major broke in, "that may be true; and so has the influence of the other churches. But what I want to know is this: How can you protect a negro here more than you protect an Italian in the North?"

"My dear sir, the Italian in the North is protected."

"I grant you, but by the law rather than by the church."

"But is not the church behind the law?" There was a shrewd twinkle in the priest's eyes, and he was about to proceed with his talk when old Gid snorted: "I gad, I hear that the public schools of the North are in the hands of the Catholics, and if that's the case I reckon they've got a pretty good hold on the court house. I understand that they daresn't open a Bible in the public schools of Chicago; and they also tell me that the children there have to learn Dutch. Zounds, ain't that enough to make old Andy Jackson rattle his bones in his grave? I wish I had my way for a few weeks. I'd show the world that this is America. I'd catch low-browed wretches carrying all sorts of spotted and grid-ironed flags through the streets. Dutch! Now, I'd just like to hear a child of mine gabbling Dutch."

The priest addressed himself to the Major: "You ask how we are to protect the negro in the South. I will tell you—by teaching him that except in the Catholic Church he cannot hope to find perfect equality. Our communion knows no color—save red, and that is the blood of Christ. Our religion is the only true democracy, but a democracy which teaches that a man must respect himself before he should expect others to respect him. But, my dear Major, I am not here to convince you, but to convince the negro. He has been buffeted about by political parties, and now it remains for the church to save him. One of these days an act rather than a word may convince you."

Tom had come out upon the porch. For a time he stood, listening, then quickly stepping down into the yard, he gazed toward the dairy house, into which, accompanied by a negro woman, had gone a slim girl, wearing a gingham sun-bonnet. The girl came out, carrying a jug, and hastened toward the yard gate. Tom heard the gate-latch click and then stepped quickly to the corner of the house; and when out of sight he almost ran to overtake the girl. She had reached the road, and she pretended to walk faster when she heard his footsteps. She did not raise her eyes as he came up beside her.

"Let me carry the jug, Sallie."

"No, I can carry it."

"Give it to me."

He took the jug and she looked up at him with a smile.

"How's your uncle, Sallie?"

"He ain't any better."

Her uncle was Wash Sanders. Twenty years had passed since he had first issued a bulletin that he was dying. He had liver trouble and a strong combination of other ailments, but he kept on living. At first the neighbors had confidence in him, and believed that he was about to pass away, but as the weeks were stretched into years, as men who had been strong and hearty were one by one borne to the grave, they began to lose faith in Wash Sanders. All day long he would sit on his shaky verandah, built high off the ground, and in answer to questions concerning his health would answer: "Can't keep up much longer; didn't sleep a wink last night. Don't eat enough to keep a chicken alive." His cows appeared always to be dry, and every day he would send his niece, Sallie Pruitt, for a jug of buttermilk. He had but one industry, the tending and scraping of a long nail on the little finger of his left hand. He had a wife, but no children. His niece had recently come from the pine woods of Georgia. Her hair looked like hackled flax and her eyes were large and gray.

"I didn't think you could see me," said the girl, taking off her bonnet and swinging it as she walked, keeping a sort of time with it.

"Why, you couldn't possibly come and get away without my

seeing you."

"Yes, I could if it was night."

"Not much. I could see you in the dark, you are so bright."

"I'm not anything of the sort. Give me the jug and let me go on by myself if you are goin' to make fun of me."

She reached for the jug and he caught her hand, and walking along, held it.

"I wouldn't want to hold anybody's hand that I'd made fun of," she said, striving, though gently, to pull it away.

"I didn't make fun of you. I said you were bright and you are. To me you are the brightest thing in the world. Whenever I dream of you I awake with my eyes dazzled."

"Oh, you don't, no such of a thing."

They saw a wagon coming, and he dropped her hand. He stepped to the right, she to the left, and the wagon passed between them. She looked at him in alarm. "That's bad luck," she said.

"What is?"

"To let anything pass between us."

"Oh, it doesn't make any difference."

"Yes, it does," she insisted. "No, you mustn't take my hand again—you've let something pass between us."

He awkwardly grabbed after her hand. She held it behind

her, and about her waist he pressed his arm. "Oh, don't do that. Somebody might see us."

"I don't care if the whole world sees us."

"You say that now, but after awhile you'll care."

"Never as long as I live. You know I love you."

"No, I don't."

"Yes, you do."

"You might say you do, but you don't. But even if you do love me now you won't always."

"Yes, as long as I live."

She looked up at him, and her eyes were full of beauty and tenderness. "Your mother—"

"None of that," he broke in. "I am my own master. To me you are the most beautiful creature in the world, and—"

"Somebody's comin'," she said.

A horseman came round a bend in the road, and he stepped off from her, but they did not permit the horseman to pass between them. He did not put his arm about her again, for now they were within sight of her uncle's desolate house. They saw Wash Sanders sitting on the verandah. Tom carried the jug as far as the yard gate.

"Won't you come in?" Sanders called.

"I ought to be getting back, I guess."

"Might come in and rest awhile."

Tom hesitated a moment and then passed through the gate. The girl had run into the house.

"How are you getting along?" the young man asked as he began slowly to tramp up the steps.

"Porely, mighty porely. Thought I was gone last night—didn't sleep a wink. And I don't eat enough to keep a chicken alive."

"Wouldn't you like a mess of young squirrels?" Tom asked, as he sat down in a hickory rocking chair. Of late he had become interested in Wash Sanders, and had resented the neighbors' loss of confidence in him.

"Well, you might bring 'em if it ain't too much trouble, but I don't believe I could eat 'em. Don't eat enough to keep a chicken alive."

He lifted his pale hand, and with his long finger nail scratched his chin.

"What's the doctor's opinion?" Tom asked, not knowing what else to say and feeling that at that moment some expression was justly demanded of him.

"The doctors don't say anything now; they've given me up. From the first they saw that I was a dead man. Last doctor that gave me medicine was a fellow from over here at Gum Springs, and I wish I may die dead if he didn't come in one of finishin' me right there on the spot."

There came a tap at a window that opened out upon the verandah, and the young fellow, looking around, saw the girl sitting in the "best room." She tried to put on the appearance of having accidentally attracted his attention. He moved his chair closer to the window.

"How did you know I was in here?" she asked, looping back the white curtain.

"I can always tell where you are without looking."

"Are you goin' to make fun of me again?"

"If I could even eat enough to keep a chicken alive I think I'd feel better," said Wash Sanders, looking far off down the road.

"I never did make fun of you," the young fellow declared in a whisper, leaning close to the window. "And I wish you wouldn't keep on saying that I do."

"I won't say it any more if you don't want me to."

"But I can't eat and can't sleep, and that settles it," said Wash Sanders.

"Of course I don't want you to say it. It makes me think that you are looking for an excuse not to like me."

"Would you care very much if I didn't like you?"

"If I had taken another slug of that Gum Springs doctor's stuff I couldn't have lived ten minutes longer," said Wash Sanders.

And thus they talked until the sun was sinking into the tops of the trees, far down below the bend in the river.

CHAPTER VII

At the Major's house the argument was still warm and vigorous. But the evening was come, and the bell-cow, home from her browsing, was ringing for admittance at the barn-yard gate. The priest arose to go. At that moment there was a heavy step at the end of the porch, the slow and ponderous tread of Jim Taylor. He strode in the shadow and in the gathering dusk recognition of him would not have been easy, but by his bulk and height they knew him. But he appeared to have lost a part of his great strength, and he drooped as he walked.

"Where is the Major?" he asked, and his voice was hoarse.

"Here, my boy. Why, what's the trouble?"

"Let me see you a moment," he said, halting.

The Major arose, and the giant, with one stride forward, caught him by the arm and led him away amid the black shadows under the trees. Mrs. Cranceford came out upon the porch and stood looking with cool disapproval upon the priest. At a window she had sat and heard him enunciate his views. Out in the yard Jim Taylor said something in a broken voice, and the Major, madly bellowing, came bounding toward the house.

"Margaret," he cried, "Louise is married!"

The woman started, uttered not a sound, but hastening to meet him, took him by the hand. Jim Taylor came ponderously walking from amid the black shadows. The Englishman and old Gid stole away. The priest stood calmly looking upon the old man and his wife.

"John, come and sit down," she said. "Raving won't do any good. We must be seemly, whatever we are." She felt the eye of the priest. "Who told you, Mr. Taylor?"

"The justice of the peace. They were married about an hour ago, less than half a mile from here."

She led the Major to a chair, and he sat down heavily. "She shall never darken my door again," he declared, striving to stiffen his shoulders, but they drooped under his effort.

"Don't say that, dear; don't say that. It is so cold and cruel."

"But I do say it—ungrateful little wretch. It rises up within me and I can't keep from saying it."

The priest stepped forward and raised his hand. "May the blessings of our Heavenly Father rest upon this household," he said. The woman looked a defiance at him. He bowed and was gone. Jim Taylor stood with his head hung low. Slowly he began to speak. "Major, you and your wife are humiliated, but I am heart-broken. You are afflicted with a sorrow, but I am struck down with grief. But I beg of you not to say that she shan't come home again. Her marriage doesn't alter the fact that she is your daughter. Her relationship toward you may not be so much changed, but to me she is lost. I beg you not to say she shan't come home again."

Mrs. Cranceford tenderly placed her hand on the giant's arm. He shook under her touch.

"I will say it and I mean it. She has put her feet on our love and has thrown herself away, and I don't want to see her again. I do think she is the completest fool I ever saw in my life. Yes, and we loved her so. And Tom—it will break his heart."

In the dusk the wife's white hand was gleaming—putting back the gray hair from her husband's eyes. "And we still love her so, dear," she said.

"What!" he cried, and now his shoulders stiffened. "What! do you uphold her?"

"Oh, no, but I am sorry for her, and I am not going to turn against her simply because she has made a mistake. She has acted unwisely, but she has not disgraced herself."

"Yes, she has disgraced herself and the rest of us along with her. She has married the dying son of a convict. I didn't want to tell you this—I told her—"

This was like a slap in the face, and for a moment she was bereft of the cool dignity that had been so pronounced a characteristic of her quiet life.

"If you didn't tell me before why do you tell me now?" was her reply. She stood back from him, regathering her scattered reserve, striving to be calm. "But it can't be helped now, John." Her gentle dignity reasserted itself. "Let time and the something that brightens hopes and softens fears gradually soothe our affliction."

She had taken up the Major's manner of speech. "Mr. Taylor,

I have never intimated such a thing to you before," she added, "but it was my hope that she might become your wife. There, my dear man, don't let it tear you so."

The giant was shaken, appearing to be gnarled and twisted by her words, like a tree in a fierce wind. "I talked to her about you," she continued, "and it was my hope—but now let us be kind to her memory, if indeed we are to regard her simply as a memory."

"Margaret," said the Major, getting up and throwing back his leonine head, "you are enough to inspire me with strength—you always have. But while you may teach me to bear a trouble, you can't influence me to turn counter to the demands of a just resentment. She shan't put her foot in this house again. Jim, you can find a more suitable woman, sir. Did you hear what became of them after that scoundrel married them? Who performed the ceremony? Morris? He must never put his foot in my yard again. I'll set the dogs on him. What became of them, Jim?"

"I didn't hear, but I think that they must have driven to town in a buggy."

"Well, it really makes no difference what became of them. Are you going, Jim?"

"Yes, sir."

"Won't you stay with us to-night?"

"No, I thank you. It's better for me to be alone." He hesitated. "If you want me to I'll find out to-night where they've gone."

"Oh, no, do nothing of the sort, for I assure you that it makes no difference. Let them go to the devil."

"John, don't say that, please," his wife pleaded.

"But I have said it. Well, if you are determined to go, good-night."

"Good-night." Jim strode off into the darkness, but halted and turned about. "Major, if I can forgive her you ought to," he said. "You've got common sense to help you, but common sense was never known to help a man that's in my fix."

They heard the gate open, heard the latch click behind him as he passed out into the road. Toward his lonely home he trod his heavy way, in the sand, in the rank weeds, picking not his course, stumbling, falling once to his knees. The air was full of the pungent scent of the walnut, turning yellow, and in it was a memory of Louise. Often had he seen her with her apron full of nuts that had fallen from the trees under which he now was passing. He halted and looked about him. The moon was rising and he saw some one sitting on a fence close by the road side. "Is that you, Jim?" a voice called.

"Yes. Oh, it's you, is it, Mr. Batts?"

"Yep, just about. Hopped up here to smell the walnuts. Takes me away back. They took it pretty hard, didn't they?"

"Yes, particularly the Major. His wife has more control over herself."

"Or may be less affection," Gid replied. "They say she's strong, but I call her cold. Hold on and I'll walk with you." He got down off the fence and walked beside the giant. "She's a mighty strange woman to me," the old man said when they had walked for a time in silence. "But there's no question of the fact that she's strong, that is, as some people understand strength. To me, I gad, there is more force in affection than in restraint. She loves her children—no doubt about that—and of course she thinks the world of the Major, but somehow she misjudges people. She doesn't understand me at all. But I reckon the majority of men are too deep for a woman. I didn't want to see them in the throes of their trouble, and I says to the Englishman, 'it's time to git,' and we got. He wanted me to go over to his house and get some Scotch whisky. I told him that the last rain must have left some water in a hollow stump near my house, and that I preferred it to his out-landish drink. And hanged if he didn't think I was in earnest. Yes, sir, I knew that girl would marry him; and let me tell you, if I was a youngster I would rather have her love than the love of any woman I ever saw. There's something about her I never saw in any other woman—I gad, she's got character; understand me? She ain't beautiful, hardly handsome, but there's something about her, hanged if I know what it is. But it's something; and I've always found that the strongest charm about a woman is a something that you can't exactly catch—something that is constantly on the dodge. And you bet I've had lots of experience. The Major could tell you many a story on me. Yes, sir. Say, Jim, I know how you feel over this affair, and I want you to understand that I'm your friend, first, last and all the time. I've been trying to talk up to the right place, but now I don't exactly know what to say."

"Don't say anything, Uncle Gideon."

"I reckon that would be about the wisest plan. Just wanted to let you know where to find me. Strange things happen even in this quiet community, don't they? But I'm woefully sorry that this special thing has happened. I gad, the Major snorted so loud that my horse broke loose from the post, and that's the reason I'm stepping around here like a blind dog in a meat house. Begin pickin' to-morrow, I reckon?"

"I don't know. I had made all my arrangements, but now after what's happened I don't care whether there's a boll picked or not. I'm let down."

"Don't feel that way, old fellow. You'll be all right in a day or two."

"Mr. Batts, if I didn't know that you were trying to soothe me I would take that remark as an insult. If I thought I wasn't any more steadfast than to be all right in a day or two—if I really believed my character that light, I swear I'd go this minute and drown myself."

"Why, my dear boy, you know I didn't mean to infer that your heart had no more memory than that. What I meant was that your sense of resignation would demand a hearing, so to speak. Let me tell you something. I understand that girl better than her father or mother does—I have made her a special study, and I want to tell you that when I take the trouble to throw my mind on a woman a mystery has to be cleared right then and there. And this is what I want to say: She has married that fellow out of pity. I don't believe she loves him. Always was ruled by pity. Recollect hearing the Major tell of a sudden streak of misfortune that overtook his family when he was a child. His father had to sell several of his slaves, and his old black mammy stood on the block with him in her arms while they were auctioning her off. Well, sir, Louise cried about that fit to kill herself. We told her how long ago it had happened, and impressed on her the fact that the old woman was soon bought back, but she kept on crying over the cruelty of the thing. Yes, sir. Well, I turn off here. Good night."

In the dark the Major walked about the yard mournfully calling Tom. A negro woman said that she had seen him going down the road, and the old gentleman returned to the porch and sat down. In the sitting room a lamp was burning, and a patch of light fell about his chair. He wanted to tell the young man of the trouble that had fallen upon the household, and yet he dreaded to hear his footstep. Tom was so proud of his sister, had always looked up to her, had regarded her whims as an intellectual diversion; and now what a disappointment. How sadly would his heart be wrung. From a distant room came the pling-plang of a banjo.

"There's Tom, Margaret. Will you please tell him to come here? I don't want to see him in the light."

Mrs. Cranceford hastened to obey, and the Major sat listening. He pushed his chair back out of the patch of light. The banjo hushed its twanging, and then he heard Tom coming. The young man stepped out upon the porch. His mother halted in the doorway.

"Tom," said the Major, "I have a desperate piece of news, and I wish I could break it to you gently, but there is no way to lead up to it. Your sister has married Carl Pennington."

"Yes, so Jim Taylor told me. Met him in the road a while ago. I didn't know that there was anything of the sort on hand. Must have kept it mighty quiet. I suppose—"

"What, you suppose! What the deuce can you suppose! Stand there supposing when I tell you that she has married a dying man." The old gentleman flounced in his chair. "She has thrown herself away and I tell you of it and you want to suppose. What's the matter with you? Have you lost all your pride and your sense? She has married a dying man, I tell you."

The young fellow began awkwardly to twist himself about. He looked at his mother, standing in the door with the light pouring about her, but her eyes were turned from him, gazing far away into the deepening night. "I know they might think he's dying," he said, "but they might be mistaken. Sometimes they believe a man's dying and he keeps on living. Wash Sanders—"

"Go back to your banjo, you idiot!" the Major shouted. "I'll swear this beats any family on the face of the earth." He got up, knocking over his chair. "Go on. Don't stand there trying to splutter an explanation of your lack of sense! No wonder you have always failed to pass an examination. Not a word, Margaret. I know what you are going to say: Beats any family on the face of the earth."

CHAPTER VIII

On the morrow there was a song and a chant in the cotton fields. Aged fingers and youthful hands were eager with grabbing the cool, dew-dampened fleece of the fields. The women wore bandana handkerchiefs, and picturesquely down the rows their red heads were bobbing. Whence came their tunes, so quaintly weird, so boisterous and yet so full of melancholy? The composer has sought to catch them, has touched them with his refining art and has spoiled them. The playwright has striven to transfer from the field to the stage a cotton-picking scene and has made a travesty of it. To transfer the passions of man and to music-riddle them is an art with stiff-jointed rules, but the charm of a cotton-picking scene is an essence, and is breathed but cannot be caught. Here seems to lie a sentiment that no other labor invites, and though old with a thousand endearments, it is ever an opera rehearsed for the first time. But this is the view that may be taken only by the sentimentalist, the poet loitering along the lane. To him it is a picture painted to delight the eye, to soothe the nerves, to inspire a pastoral ode. There is, however, another side. At the edge of the field where the cotton is weighed, stands the planter watching the scales. His commercial instincts might have been put to dreamy sleep by the appearance of the purple bloom, but it is keenly aroused by the opening boll. He is influenced by no song, by no color fantastically bobbing between the rows. He is alert, determined not to be cheated. Too much music might cover a rascally trick, might put a clod in the cotton to be weighed. Sentiment is well enough, and he can get it by turning to Walter Scott.

None of the planters was shrewder than the Major. In his community he was the business as well as the social model. He was known to be brave and was therefore expected to be generous. His good humor was regarded as an echo of his prosperity, and a lucky negro, winning at dice, would strive to imitate his manner. At planting, at plowing and at gathering, no detail was too small or too illusive to escape his eye. His interests were under a microscopic view and all plans that were drawn in the little brick office at the corner of the yard, were rigorously carried out in the fields. In the one place he was all business; in the other there was in him an admixture of good humor and executive thoroughness. He knew how many pounds of cotton a certain man or woman was likely to pick within the working hours of a day, and he marked the clean and the trashy pickers; and the play of his two-colored temperament was seen in his jovial banter of the one and his harsh reprimand of the other. But to-day a hired man stood at the scales to see the cotton weighed. The Major walked abroad throughout the fields. As he drew near, the negroes hushed their songs and their swaggering talk. They bowed respectfully to him and to one another whispered his affliction. At noon, when he returned home, the housekeeper told him that his wife was away. He sat down in the library to wait for her. Looking out he saw Sallie Pruitt carrying a jug across the yard. A few moments later he asked for Tom and was told that he had just left the house. He tried to read, but nothing interested him. There was nothing but dullness in the newspaper and even Ivanhoe had lost his charm. It was nearly three o'clock when Mrs. Cranceford returned. He did not ask whither she had gone; he waited to be told. She sat down, taking off her gloves.

"Did you see Mr. Perdue?" she asked.

"No, I have seen no one. Don't care much to see any one."

"I didn't know but you might have met him. He was here this morning. Told me about Louise."

"What does he know about her?"

"He told me where she had gone to live—in that old log house at the far end of the Anthony place."

"Well, go on, I'm listening."

"I didn't know that you cared to hear."

"Then why did you begin to tell me?"

She did not answer this question. She waited for him to say more. "Of course I'd like to know what has become of her."

"I went over to see her," said Mrs. Cranceford.

"The deuce you did."

"John, don't talk that way."

"I won't. You went to see her."

"Yes, and in that miserable house, all open, she is nursing her dying husband."

The Major got up and began to walk about the room. "Don't, Margaret, I'd rather not hear about it."

"But you must hear. No place could be more desolate. The

wind was moaning in the old plum thicket. The gate was down and hogs were rooting in the yard. Louise did not hear me as I drove up, the wind was moaning so distressfully among the dead plum bushes—she did not know that I was on the place until I entered the room where she sat at the bedside of her husband. She jumped up with a cry and—"

"Margaret, please don't."

"I must tell you, John. I will tell you. She jumped up with a cry and ran to me, and started to take off my cloak, but remembering that there was no fire in the damp room, she let it stay on. She tried to speak, but couldn't. Her husband held out his waxen hand, and when I took it I shuddered with the cold chill it sent through me."

"Margaret, I am going out," said the Major, turning toward the door.

"If you do, John, I will go with you and tell you as we walk along. Please sit down."

He sat down with an air of helplessness. He fumbled with his fingers, which seemed to have grown thicker; he moved his foot as if it were a heavy weight. His wife continued: "In the room there was scarcely any furniture, nothing to soften the appearance of bleakness. I asked why no fire had been made, and Louise said that she had engaged a negro to cut some wood, but that he had gone away. She had paid him in advance. She would herself have kindled a fire, but there was no axe on the place, and she was afraid to leave her husband long enough to go to the woods to gather sticks. I went out and found the negro dozing in the sun. He was impudent when I spoke to him, but when I told him my name and threatened him with you, he scuffled to his feet and sauntered off, and I thought that we should see no more of him, but soon we heard the lazy strokes of his axe. And shortly afterward we had a fire. Louise was in one of her silent moods, but Pennington talked as much as his cough would permit him. He said that it was all his fault. 'I told her,' said he, 'that unless she married me I would die blaspheming the name of God, and that if she would save me from hell she must be my wife. I know that it was selfish and mean, but I couldn't help it. And so she has married me to save my soul.' He grew excited and I tried to calm him. I told him that you were angry at first, but that now you were in a better humor toward him."

"Margaret—"

"This appeared to help him, but I saw that Louise did not believe me. However, I commanded her to come home and bring her husband with her. But she shook her head and declared that she would never again enter your house until she could in some way discharge the debt of gratitude with which you reproached her, which she says you flaunted in her face at a time when she was greatly distressed."

"What! I don't exactly understand."

"Yes, you do, dear. You reminded her that you had saved her life, and told her that you based your plea for obedience upon your own gallantry."

"Oh, that was a piece of mere nonsense, a theatrical trick. Of course I don't deserve any credit for having saved the life of my own child."

"It may have been a theatrical trick with you, but it wasn't with her. She keenly feels your reproach."

"Confound it, you are both making a monster of me."

"No, dear, that is not our design."

"Our design! Have you too, set yourself against me? Let me go to old Gideon. He's the only friend I've got."

"John, you mustn't say that. And why, at this time, should you refer to that old sinner? But let me go on. While I was there the doctor came, and shortly afterward we heard a heavy tread on the flapping boards of the passageway that divides the two sections of the old house."

"Jim Taylor," said the Major.

"Yes, Jim Taylor. Louise jumped up in a flutter. He didn't take any notice of her excitement. 'I heard that you were living here,' he said, 'and knowing what sort of an old place it is, I've come to see if I can be of any use to you.' Here he looked about at the cracks in the walls and the holes in the roof. 'And you'll pardon me,' he went on, 'but I took the liberty to bring a carpenter along to patch up things a little. That's him out there at work on the gate.' Louise began to cry. He pretended not to notice her. 'It won't take long to make this a very comfortable place,' he went on, 'and I hope you won't feel offended, but I have brought some young chickens and a squirrel or two—in a basket out there in the kitchen. I always was a sort of a neighborly fellow you know.' 'You are the best man in the world,' Louise broke out. 'No, not in the world, but I reckon I can stand flat-footed and lift with the most of them,' he replied, assuming that he thought she referred to his strength. 'Yes,' he continued, 'and the boys will be here pretty soon with the wagon to haul you some wood. And I hope you'll pardon me again, but nothing would do old Aunt Nan but she must come over to cook for you and help you take care of Mr. Pennington until he gets about again. She's the best cook in the whole country. You know the governor of the state once said that she could beat anybody frying a chicken, and—'"

"Confound his impudence!" exclaimed the Major, grinding the floor as he wheeled about, "he's performing the offices that belong to me. And I won't stand it."

"The offices that did belong to you, dear, but you have washed your hands of them."

"Have I? Well, we'll see about that. I'll send over there and have everything put to rights. No, I'll send the carriage and have them brought home. I'll be—I say I won't be made a scape-goat of in this way. Why, confound—"

"John."

"Yes, I understand, but I won't put up with it any longer. I'll send Tom over there—I'll send the law over there and bring them home under arrest."

She shook her head. "No, it will be of no use to send for them. Louise will not come, and you know she won't. Besides, we can make her just as comfortable there as here. It will not be for long, so let her have her own way."

"By the blood, she has had it!"

"John, have you forgotten that you are a member of the church?"

"That's all right. But do you mean by member of the church that I am to draw in my head like a high-land terrapin every time anything is said to me? Am I to be brow-beaten by everybody just because I belong to the church? Oh, it's a happy day for a woman when she can squash her husband with the church. I gad, it seems that all a married woman wants with a church is to hit her husband on the head with it."

"John, now you are the echo of old Gid."

"I'm not and you know it, but there are times when a man would be excusable for being the echo of the devil. But for gracious sake don't cry. Enough to make a man butt his head against the wall. Just as a man thinks a woman is stronger than a lion she tunes up and cries. There, Margaret, let it all go. There." He put his arm about her. "Everything will come out all right. I am wrong and I confess it. I am bull-headed and as mean as a dog."

"No, you are not," she protested, wiping her eyes.

"Yes, I am and I see it now. You are always right. And you may manage this affair just as you see fit. Poor little girl. But never mind, it will all come right. Let us walk down the lane. It is beautiful down there. The frost has painted things up for you; the sumac bushes are flaming and the running briars on the fences are streams of fire. Come on." He took her by the hand and led her away.

CHAPTER IX

Within a few days a great change was wrought in the appearance of the old log house. The roof, which had been humped in the middle like the back of a lean, acorn-hunting hog, was straightened and reshingled; the yard was enclosed with a neat fence; and the stack chimney which had leaned off from the house as if it would fall, was shoved back and held in place with strong iron bands. And the interior was transformed. Soft carpets were spread, easy chairs provided, the rough walls were papered and the windows were curtained. The fire-light fell upon pictures, and a cat had come to take her place at the corner of the hearth; but in the dead of night, when all the birds were hushed, when the wind moaned in the plum thicket, the hollow and distressing cough echoed throughout the house. At evening sorrowful-looking cows would come down the lane, and standing at the gate would low mournfully, an attention which they ever seek to pay a dismal place, but Jim Taylor entered a complaint, threatened violence and finally compelled their owners to have them driven home before the arrival of their time for lonesome lowing. It was Jim's custom to call at morning and at evening. Sometimes, after looking about the place, he would merely come to the door and ask after Mr. Pennington and then go away.

One morning when Louise answered his tap at the door, she

told him that the sufferer was much better and that she believed he was going to get well.

"I'm mighty glad to hear it," he replied. "The doctors can't always tell."

"Won't you come in?"

"No, I might worry him."

"Oh, not in the least. He's asleep anyway, and I'm lonesome. Come in, please."

He followed her into the house, trying to lessen his weight as if he were walking on thin ice; and the old house cracked its knuckles, but his foot-fall made not a sound. She placed a chair for him and sat down with her hands in her lap, and how expressive they were, small and thin, but shapely. She was pale and neat in a black gown. To him she had never looked so frail, and her eyes had never appeared so deeply blue, but her hands—he could not keep his eyes off them—one holding pity and the other full of appeal.

"Don't you need a little more wood on?" he asked.

"No, it's not cold enough for much fire."

"Where did you get that cat?"

"She came crying around the other day and I let her in, and she has made herself at home."

"The negroes say it's good luck for a cat to come to the house." She sighed. "I don't believe in luck."

"I do. I believe in bad luck, for it's generally with me. Does your mother come every day?"

"Yes, although I beg her not to."

"I reckon she'll do about what she wants to. Has the Major—"

She held up her hand and he sat looking at her with his mouth half open. But at the risk of offending her, he added: "I didn't know but he might have come over."

"He would, but I won't let him."

"And do you think it's exactly right not to let him?"

"I think it is exactly right to do as a something within me dictates," she answered. "He placed me in a certain position—"

"But he is more than willing to take you out of it," Taylor broke in. "He doesn't want you to remain in that position."

"No, he can't take me out of it. He charged me with ingratitude, and I would rather he had driven me off the place. Nothing can be much crueler than to remind one of ingratitude; it is like shooting from behind a rock; it is having one completely at your mercy."

Now she sat leaning forward with her hands clasped over her knees. Pennington coughed slightly in his sleep and she looked toward the bed. She straightened up and put the hair back out of her eyes and Taylor followed the motion of her hand.

"Did he eat the squirrel?"

"Yes, and enjoyed it."

The cat got up, stretched, and rubbing against the tongs, knocked them down with a clatter. Pennington awoke. Louise was beside him in a moment. "Ah, it's you, Mr. Taylor," he said.

"Yes, but it wasn't me that made the noise."

"Oh, it didn't disturb me, I assure you. I was just about waking up anyway. That will do, thank you." Louise had begun to arrange the pillows. "I'll sit up. See how strong I am. Give me a pipe. I believe I can smoke a little."

She went to fill a pipe for him, and turning to Taylor, he said: "I'm getting stronger now every day; good appetite, sleep first-rate. And I'll be able to walk about pretty soon. Oh, they had me dead, you know, but I knew better all the time."

Louise placed a coal upon his pipe and handed it to him. She said that she was afraid it might make him cough, but it did not.

"I have always maintained that there was nothing the matter with my lungs," he said, contentedly blowing rings of smoke. "Why, I hadn't a symptom of consumption except the cough, and that's about gone. And my prospects were never better than they are this minute. Received a letter yesterday from over in Alabama—want me to take a professorship in a college. The first thing you know I shall have charge of the entire institution. And when I get up in the world I want it understood, Mr. Taylor, that I shall never forget you. Your kindness—"

"Don't speak of it," Taylor put in, holding up his hand in imitation of Louise. "I've known this little lady, sir, all her life, and I'd be a brute to forget her in time of trouble."

"Yon are a true-hearted man, Mr. Taylor, and I shall never forget you, sir." And after a short silence, he added: "All I desire is a chance, for with it, I can make Louise happy. I need but little money, I should not know how to disport a large fortune, but I do desire a comfortable home with pictures and books. And I thank the Lord that I appreciate the refinements of this life." In silence he smoked, looking up at the rings. "Ah, but it was dark for me a short time ago, Mr. Taylor. They made me believe that I was going to die. We hear a great deal of resignation, of men who welcome the approach of death, but I was in despair. And looking upon a strong man, a man whose strength was thrown upon him, a man who had never thought to take even the slightest care of himself, I was torn with blasphemous rage. It wasn't right. But thank God, I lived through that dark period, and am now getting well. Don't you think so?"

"Why, yes, I can see it. And I'll tell you what we'll do: I'll bring over the dogs pretty soon and we'll go hunting. How does that strike you?"

Pennington propped himself higher in the bed and put his pipe on a chair. "It has been a long time since I went hunting," he said, musingly. "It seems a long time since I have done anything, except to brood over my failing health. But I will have no more of that. Yes, I will go hunting with you." He shoved up the sleeve of his shirt and called his wife's attention. "Don't you think I'm getting more flesh on my arm? Look here. No dying man has this much muscle. Louise, I'm going to get up. There is really no use of my lying here."

He threw off the covers and the giant arose and stood looking upon him, smiling sadly. He asked for his clothes, and when Louise had brought them he picked at a worn spot and said: "I must get some clothes with the first money I earn. I didn't know that this coat was so far gone. Why, look, it is almost threadbare; and the trousers are not much better. Let a man get sick and he feels that the world is against him; let him get well and wear poor clothes, and he will find that the world doesn't think enough of him to set itself against him—find that the world does not know him at all."

Taylor ventured upon the raveled platitude that clothes do not make the man. Pennington shook his head, still examining his trousers. "That will do in a copy-book, but not in life," said he. And then looking up as Taylor moved toward the door, he asked: "Are you going?"

"Yes, I must get back to see how things are getting along. Be over again to-morrow."

Louise went with him out into the passage. He halted at the log step and stood there, looking at her. "Mr. Taylor, I can never forget your kindness," she said.

"All right, but I hope you won't remember to mention it again."

He looked at her hands, looked into her eyes; and frankly she returned his gaze, for it was a gaze long and questioning.

"Your friendship—" he held up his hand to stop her. "Won't you let me speak of that, either?"

"You may speak of it, but you must know that it does not exist," he answered, leaning against a corner of the house, still looking at her.

"But you don't mean that you are not my friend?"

"I mean what I told you some time ago—that there can be no

friendship between a big man and a little woman."

"Oh, I had forgotten that."

"No, you hadn't; you thought of it just then as you spoke."

"Why, Mr. Taylor, how can you say that?"

"I can say it because it is true. No, there can be no friendship between us."

"You surely don't mean that there can be anything else." She had drawn back from him and was stiffly erect with her arms folded, her head high; and so narrow was the hard look she gave him that her eyes appeared smaller. Her lips were so tightly compressed that dimples showed in her cheeks; and thus with nature's soft relics of babyhood, she denied her own resentment.

"On your part I don't presume that there can be anything else," he answered, speaking the words slowly, as if he would weigh them one at a time on the tip of his tongue. "You may think of me as you please, as circumstances now compel you to think, and I will think of you not as I please, but as I must."

"Please don't talk that way. Don't reproach me when I am in such need of—of friendship. One of these days you may know me better, but now you can regard me only as a freak. Yes, I am a freak."

"You are an angel."

"Mr. Taylor!" Again her head was high, and in her eyes was the same suggestion of a sharp squint.

"You didn't tell me that I shouldn't think of you as I please."

"But I didn't tell you to speak what you might be pleased to think. There, Carl is calling me. Good-bye."

CHAPTER X

Jim Taylor, too humane to impose the burden of his weight upon a horse, always made his visits on foot, and this day while trudging homeward, he met Mrs. Cranceford. She had of late conceived so marked a sympathy for him, that her manner toward him was warmly gentle.

Taylor stepped to the road-side and halted there as she drove up alone in a buggy. With a sorrowful reverence he took off his hat, and she smiled sympathetically; and the lazy old horse, appearing to understand it all, stopped of his own accord.

"Good morning, Jim. Have you been over to the house?"

"Yes, ma'm, just left there."

"How is he?"

"So much better that I believe he's going to get well."

"You don't say so! Why, I am—" she was about to say that she was delighted to hear it, but on the giant's face she thought she saw a deeper shadow lying, heard in his voice a softer note of sorrow; and considerately she checked her intended utterance. Then they looked at each other and were ashamed.

"He was up dressing himself when I left."

"You surprise me."

"And he has surprised us all, ma'm. I don't believe he's got consumption; his cough has left him. Why, he's thinking of taking a place in a college over in Alabama."

"He is? But I hope he won't take Louise so far from home."

He shifted his position and sunk his hands deep into his pockets. "I guess he thinks she can't be so very far from home as long as she is with him."

"But it makes no difference what he thinks." Mrs. Cranceford persisted. "He must not take her over there. Why, I should think he could find employment here." Jim looked far away, and she added: "Is your cotton turning out well?"

"First-rate, and I want to sell it as soon as I can. I've got to go away."

"Go away!" she repeated. "You don't mean it?"

"Yes, ma'm, I do. If he gets well they won't have any more use for me and I might as well go off somewhere and take a fresh start; and besides, I can't keep from showing that I love her, and no matter how cool she might be toward me it couldn't help but pain him. And there are people in this neighborhood mean enough to talk about it: No longer ago than yesterday that strapping Alf Joyner threw out a hint of this sort, and although he meant it in fun, maybe, I snatched him off the fence where he was sitting, and walloped him in the road. No, I can't keep from showing how much I think of her; there is so much of me," he added, with a smile, "that I can't be a hypercrite all over at once."

At this she smiled, but her countenance grew serious and she said:

"I am sorry you have been compelled to resent an insinuation." She gathered up the lines. "But perhaps you imagine more than is intended. It is easy, and also natural that you should."

Jim made no reply. She bowed to him, shook the lines, and the old horse moved on. Just before reaching a bend in the road, she looked back at him. How powerful was his bearing, how strong his stride; and with all his bigness he was not ungraceful.

Everywhere, in the fields, along the fences, lay October's wasteful ripeness, but the season was about to turn, for the bleak corner of November was in sight. A sharp wind blew out of a cloud that hung low over the river, and far away against the darkening sky was a gray triangle traced, the flight of wild geese from the north. With the stiffening and the lagging of the breeze came lower and then louder the puffing of a cotton gin.

Under a persimmon tree Jim Taylor halted, and with his arms resting on a fence he stood dreamily looking across a field. Afar off the cotton pickers were bobbing between the rows. The scene was more dull than bright; to a stranger it would have been dreary, the dead level, the lone buzzard away over yonder, sailing above the tops of the ragged trees; but for this man the view was overspread with a memory of childhood. He was meditating upon leaving his home; he felt that his departure was demanded. And yet he knew that not elsewhere could he find contentment. Amid such scenes he had been born and reared. He was like the deer—would rather feed upon the rough oak foliage of a native forest than to feast upon the rich grasses of a strange land. But he had made up his mind to go. He had heard of the charm of the hills, the valleys and the streams in the northern part of the state, and once he had gone thither to acquaint himself with that paradise, but in disappointment he had come back, bringing the opinion that the people were cold and unconcerned in the comfort and the welfare of a stranger. So, with this experience fresh in his mind, he was resolved not to re-settle in his own commonwealth, but to go to a city, though feeling his unfitness for urban life. But he thought, as so many men and women have been forced to think, that life in a crowd would invite forgetfulness, that his slow broodings would find a swift flow into the tide that swallows the sad thoughts of men.

A sudden noise in the road broke the web of his musing, and looking about, he recognized Low, the Englishman. Between his teeth the Briton held his straight-stem pipe, and on his shoulder he carried his bath tub.

"Moving?" Taylor asked.

"Ah, good morning. No—not moving. An outrage has been committed. During the night someone punched a hole in the bottom of my bath. Don't know who could have done it; most extraordinary, I assure you. One of those ungrateful blacks, I warrant. Going this way? I shall be glad of your company. Ah, do you happen to know of a tinker?" he asked, as together they walked along the road.

"A what?"

"A tinker to mend my bath?"

"Haven't any such thing about here, but I guess the blacksmith can mend your tub. Here, let me carry it for you a ways. You must be tired of it by this time."

He protested, but Taylor took the tub. "Thank you. You are very kind, I'm sure. I would have sent it, but these rascals are so untrustworthy. Ah, how long do you conjecture it would take one to make his fortune in this community?"

"It depends more upon the man than the community," Taylor answered. "I know one that never could."

"And by Jove, I fancy I have a very intimate acquaintance with another. But I rather like it here, you know. I have plenty of room and no one is much disposed to interfere with me except those rascally blacks, and upon my honor I believe they tried to ruin my bath. Don't you think you'd better let me take it now?"

"No; I'll carry it. Wouldn't have known I had it if you hadn't reminded me."

"You are very kind, I'm sure. Ah, by the way, a very singular man called on me yesterday. Mayo, I believe, is his name."

"Yes, we know him down here. Came very near getting a dose of rope once. He tries to be a Moses among the negroes, but instead of leading them out of the wilderness he's going to lead them into trouble."

"I dare say as much, if they listen to him. But he avers that he doesn't want an office—wants only to see that the blacks get what they are entitled to."

"And about the first thing that will be done for him after he gets what he's entitled to," Jim replied, "will be the sending of his measure to a coffin maker."

"I surmise as much, I assure you. I didn't encourage him to prolong his visit; indeed, I told him that I preferred to be alone."

They turned out of the lane into a wood, crossed a bayou, and pursuing their way a short distance further, Taylor halted, and handing the Englishman his tub, pointed to a path that crossed the road. "That will take you to the blacksmith shop," he said.

"Ah, you are very kind," Low replied, shouldering his treasure. He turned down the path, but after going a short distance stopped and faced about. "I say, there!" he cried. "Oh, Taylor. Just a moment. I wouldn't mind having you over any evening, you know. You are a devilish decent fellow."

"All right; you may look for me most any time. Take you out 'possum hunting some night."

Low was now humping himself down the path, and Taylor turned to pursue his way homeward, when once more the Englishman faced about and shouted: "You are very kind, I'm sure. I shall be delighted."

Jim Taylor was master of a small plantation and sole inhabiter of the house wherein he was born. In the garden, under a weeping-willow tree, were the graves of his parents and of his sister, a little girl, recalled with emotion—at night when a high wind was blowing, for she had ever been afraid of a storm; and she died on a day when a fierce gale up the river blew down a cottonwood tree in the yard. She and Louise were as sisters. At her grave the giant often sat, for she was a timid little creature, afraid to be alone; and sometimes at night when the wind was hard, when a cutting sleet was driving, he would get out of his bed and stand under the tree to be near her. It was so foolishly sentimental of so strong a man that he would not have dared to tell anyone, but to the child in the grave he told his troubles. So, on this morning, when the wind was gathering its forces as it swept the fields, as the clouds were thickening far away among the whitish tops of the dead cypress trees, he went straightway to the weeping-willow, passed the grave of his father, his mother, and sat down beside the stone that bore the name and the age of the little one.

CHAPTER XI

When Mrs. Cranceford returned home early in the afternoon, she told the Major, whom she found pacing up and down the long porch, that Pennington was up and walking about the house. She told him, also, that he was resolved upon taking Louise to Alabama, and added that she herself would oppose this determination up to the very moment of departure.

The Major grunted. "What right have you to do that?" he asked. "Why should you meddle with the affairs of a man that is seeking to make a living for his wife?"

"John, you are laughing at me and I know it. Here lately you make light of everything I say."

The season was changing, he felt its influence, and he shook with good humor as he walked.

"John, you are so tickled that you can't answer me."

"Why, I could answer you very easily if I only knew what you want me to say."

This broke her whimsical resentment of his droll playfulness; she laughed with him, and taking his arm, walked up and down the porch. They talked of many things—of Louise's persistent stubbornness, and of a growing change in the conduct of Tom—his abstraction and his gentleness. He had left uncut the leaves of a sporting review, had taken to romances, and in his room had been found, sprawled on foolscap, an ill-rhymed screed in rapturous praise of soulful eyes and flaxen hair. Mrs. Cranceford knew that he must be in love; so did the Major, but he could not conjecture the object of so fervid a passion. But his wife had settled upon the object and was worried, though of her distress she had not spoken to Tom, so recent had been the discovery of the tell-tale blotch of ink. But she would as soon as an opportunity offered.

"It will soon pass," said the Major. "I don't think he intends to marry her."

"Marry her!" his wife exclaimed. "I would rather see him dead than married into a family of white trash. She may be a most amiable young person and all that, but he shan't marry her. It would break my heart, and I vow she shall never come here. Why, she came from the pine woods and is a cracker."

"But the cracker may have a most gallant and well-born origin, my dear," the Major replied. "The victim of a king's displeasure is not insignificant; he must have been a force."

"What! Do you approve of it?" she demanded, pulling away from him. "Is it possible that you would not oppose his marriage into such a family as hers must be?"

"I don't think, my dear, that her father was in the penitentiary."

"John, that is unworthy of you. I was grieved at Louise's marriage, and you know it."

In prankishness he sought a refuge; he laughed, but she did not follow him. For a moment her black eyes were hard, then came a look of distress—and tears. He put his arm about her. "Why, my dear, I didn't mean to hurt your feelings; bless your life, I didn't. Why, of course, he shan't marry her. Who ever heard of such a thing? I'll talk to him—thrash him if you say the word. There, it's all right. Why, here comes Gid."

She went into the house as Batts came up, glancing back at him as she passed through the door; and in her eyes there was nothing as soft as a tear. The old fellow winced, as he nearly always did when she gave him a direct look.

"Are you all well?" Gideon asked, lifting the tails of his long coat and seating himself in a rocking chair.

"First-rate," the Major answered, drawing forward another rocker; and when he had sat down, he added: "Somewhat of an essence of November in the air."

"Yes," Gid assented; "felt it in my joints before I got up this morning." From his pocket he took a plug of tobacco.

"I thought you'd given up chewing," said the Major. "Last time I saw you I understood you to say that you had thrown your tobacco away."

"I did, John; but, I gad, I watched pretty close where I threw it. Fellow over here gave me some stuff that he said would cure me of the appetite, and I took it until I was afraid it would, and then threw it away. I find that when a man quits tobacco he hasn't anything to look forward to. I quit for three days once, and on the third day, about the time I got up from the dinner table, I asked myself: 'Well, now, got anything to come next?' And all I could see before me was hours of hankering; and I gad, I slapped a negro boy on a horse and told him to gallop over to the store and fetch me a hunk of tobacco. And after I broke my resolution I thought I'd have a fit there in the yard waiting for that boy to come back. I don't believe that it's right for a man to kill any appetite that the Lord has given him. Of course I don't believe in the abuse of a good thing, but it's better to abuse it a little sometimes than not to have it at all. If virtue consists in deadening the nervous system to all pleasurable influences, why, you may just mark my name off the list. There was old man Haskill. I sat up with him the night after he died, and one of the men with me was harping upon the great life the old fellow had lived—never chewed, never smoked, never was drunk, never gambled, never did anything except to stand still and be virtuous—and I couldn't help but feel that he had lost nothing by dying. Haven't seen Louise, have you?"

"No; but I have about made up my mind to go over there, whether she wants me or not."

"I believe I would, John. We haven't long to stay here, and nothing sweetens our sojourn like forgiveness. I don't mean it in sacrilege, but Christ was greatest and closest to His Father when he forgave the thief."

"That's true," said the Major. "You may not be able to think very coherently, Gid, but sometimes you stroll into a discussion and bark the shins of thought."

"Easy, John. I am a thinker. My mind is full of pictures when your fancy is checkered with red and blue lines. So you are willing to forgive her?" he added after a pause.

"Yes, more than willing. But she isn't ready to be forgiven. She has some very queer notions, and I'll be hanged if I know where she picked them up. At times she's most unnatural."

"Don't say that, John. I gad, sir, what right has one person to say that another person is unnatural? Who of us is appointed to set up the standard and gauge of naturalness? Who is wholly consistent? You may say the average man. Ah, but if everyone conformed to the average there would be nothing great in the world. There is no greater bore than the well-balanced man. He wears us out with his evenness. You know what he's going to say before he says it."

"I grant you all that; but the well-balanced man made it possible for the genius to make the world great. Genius is the bloom that bursts out at the top of commonplace humanity."

"Yes, that's all very well; but just at present I'd like to have a little liquor. Be easy, though, and don't let the madam know what you're after."

"There's not a drop in the house, Gid, but there's a demijohn in the office. Let's step out there."

"No, I believe not, John," the old fellow replied, with a shudder. "Can't you bring it out?"

"She'll see me if I do. You must go with me. Whisky that's not worth going after is not worth drinking."

"You are right, John; but you have stated one of those truths that are never intended to be used except in the absence of something else that might have been said. Plain truths are tiresome, John. They never lend grace to a conversation."

"What do you know about the graces of conversation? You are better fitted to talk of the disgraces of conduct."

"Slow, John. But I know that a truth to be interesting must be whimsical or so blunt that it jolts."

"But didn't it jolt you when I said that you must go into the office after the liquor?"

"Yes; but cruelly, John. You must never jolt cruelly. I gad, I'm getting old. Do you realize that we have known each other intimately for thirty-five years?"

Mrs. Cranceford came out upon the porch. "Ah," said old Gid, without changing his tone, and as if he were continuing a moral discourse, "thirty-five years ago we heard an old circuit-rider preach at Gum Springs, and while we could not subscribe to his fiery doctrine, being inclined to the broader and more enlightened faith of the Episcopal church, yet the fervor and sincerity of his utterances made a lasting impression on us. Madam, I hear with much pleasure that Mr. Pennington is better."

"Yes, he is feeling quite improved," she replied, merely glancing at him. "Did the Major think enough of him to tell you?"

The Major looked at Gid, winked at him, and the old fellow believing that he knew what was wanted, thus answered: "Yes, ma'am, but I first heard it from the priest. He knows everything, it seems. I met him down the road and had quite a talk with him. By the way, I read a number of years ago a most edifying book, 'The Prince of the House of David.' You doubtless have it in your collection, and may I ask you to lend it to me?"

She had but small faith in the old fellow's sincerity, and yet she was pleased to see him manifest an interest in so godly a book. "Yes, and I will get it for you," she answered, going straightway to look for it; and when she had passed through the door, Gid snatched a bottle out of his pocket and held it out toward the Major. "Here, John, hurry out there and fill this up while she's gone. Meet me around at the gate. Quick!"

"Why, you old rascal, do you suppose me capable of complicity in such a fraud?"

"Oh, that's all right, John. Hurry up. I could get liquor, plenty of it, but yours always hits me where I live. I'm sick, I tell you, and hang it, I'm getting old. You don't seem to realize that I'm an old man, not long for this vain world. Take it, John, and hurry up. Confound it, you won't be deceiving her; it would be an advantage taken of her unreasonable prejudice. You never saw me drunk and never will. Thunderation, here she comes!"

He stuffed the bottle back into his hip pocket and the Major threw himself back with a loud laugh. Mrs. Cranceford, handing the book to Gid, cast a suspicious look at the Major, who continued to shake. "Why, what has amused you so?" she asked. And now old Gid was nodding and chuckling in hypocritical diversion. "I was just telling him of the first time I borrowed a copy of this book," he said. "Walked four miles to get it, and when I returned, some rascal had greased the foot-log and I slipped off into the creek. Oh, it's very funny now, but it wasn't then; had to fight to keep from losing the book and came within one of drowning. Well, I must go. Ma'am, I'm a thousand times obliged to you for this storehouse of faith, and I assure you that I'll take the best of care that it shall come back to you in good condition. By the way, John, is your office locked? I'll step out there and get that paper."

"Yes, it's locked. I'll go with you."

"Oh, never mind. Let me have the key."

"But you can't find the paper."

"Well, let it go; I can get it some other time."

The Major, slyly shaking, walked with him to the end of the porch. "You've played thunder," the old fellow whispered. "I didn't think it of you. I gad, every chance you get you hoist me on your hip and slam the life out of me. Sick as a dog, too. Again, ma'am," he added, turning about, "let me thank you for this book. And Major," he said aloud, and "damn you," he breathed, "I hope to see you over my way soon."

He swore at his horse as he mounted, and throwing back a look of reproach, he jogged off down the road. But he had not proceeded more than a mile when a boy, urging a galloping horse, overtook him and gave him a bundle; and therein he found a bottle of whisky, with these words written in red ink and pasted on the glass: "You are an old fool."

CHAPTER XII

All day the clouds had been gathering, hanging low over the fields. At evening came a downpour of rain, and at night a fitful wind was blowing—one moment of silence and then a throb of rain at the windows. In his office the Major sat, looking over the affairs of his estate. It was noted that he preferred a stormy night thus to apply himself; the harshness of figures, the unbending stubbornness of a date, in his mind seemed to find a unity with the sharp whistle of the wind and the lashes of rain on the moss-covered roof. Before him, on yellowing paper, was old Gid's name, and at it he slowly shook his head, for fretfully he nursed the consciousness of having for years been the dupe of that man's humorous rascality. The plantation was productive, the old fellow had gathered many a fine crop, and for his failure to pay rent there could be no excuse, except the apologies devised by his own trickish invention. Year after year, in his appeals for further indulgence, he had set up the plea of vague obligations pressing upon him, some old debt that he was striving to wipe out and from which he would soon be freed; and then, no longer within the tightening grasp of merciless scoundrels, he would gratefully devote the proceeds of his energies to the discharge of the obligations held so lightly over him by the noblest man on earth. Once he returned from New Orleans, whither he had gone to sell his cotton, with the story that he had been knocked senseless and robbed of his wallet, and in proof of this he produced a newspaper account of the midnight outrage, and exhibited a wound on the head, inflicted by the bludgeon of the footpad. And with such drollery did he recite this story that the Major laughed at him, which meant, of course, that his tenure of the old plantation was not to be disturbed. The memory of this rascally trick came back to the Major as he sat there looking over his papers. He recounted it all as a reminiscence of his own weakness, and he was firmly and almost angrily resolved that this season the old fellow should not waddle from under his obligations. Amusement was well enough; to laugh at a foible was harmless, but constantly to be cheated was a crime against his wife and his children. Children? Yes, for out of no calculation for the future did he leave Louise.

There came a tap at the door. Mrs. Cranceford had sent a negro boy with an umbrella and a lantern. The night was wild, and the slanting rain hit hard. Before he reached the house the wind puffed out his lantern, leaving him to stumble through the dark.

As he stepped upon the porch there was a loud "halloa" at the gate, and just at that moment he heard his wife's voice. "John, go out there and see who that is," she said.

He went round to the gate. His wife stood on the porch waiting for him. Presently he came back, walking rapidly.

"Who is it, dear?"

"A negro man. Margaret, we must go at once to Louise. Pennington is dying."

With an inarticulate note of astonishment she fled to her room, to prepare herself for the journey, and the Major loudly commanded the carriage to be brought out.

Lanterns flashed across the yard, under the streaming trees, and flickered in the gale that howled about the barn.

Pale, impatient, and wrapped in a waterproof, Mrs. Cranceford stood at the front doorway. The carriage drew up at the gate. "Are you ready?" the Major asked, speaking from the darkness in the midst of the rain.

"Yes," she answered, stepping out and closing the door.

"Where is Tom?" the Major inquired.

"He hasn't come home."

"He ought to go. I wonder where he can be."

"He could be most any place," she answered; and as she stepped under the umbrella to walk with him to the gate, she added: "But I think he is at Wash Sanders' house."

He helped her into the carriage, took a seat beside her, and shut the door with a slam. "As fast as you can!" he shouted to the driver. They sat a long time in silence, listening to the rain and the hoofs of the horses sloshing in the wet sand. The carriage stopped.

"What's the matter?"

"De bayou, sah."

"Drive on."

"De bridge is full o' holes."

"Drive through."

"De water's mighty high."

"Drive through."

Down they went with a splash. The carriage swayed, was lifted, was swung round—the horses lunged; one of the doors was burst open and the water poured in. Mrs. Cranceford clung to the Major, but she uttered not a word. Up the slippery bank the horses strained. One of them fell, but he was up in a moment. Firmer footing was gained, and the road was reached. Now they were in a lane. The Major struck a match and looked at his watch. It was nearly two o'clock. Across the fields came a light—from Louise's window.

The carriage drew up at the gate.

"That you, Major?" a voice asked.

"Yes. Why, how did you get here, Jim?"

"Tore down the fences and rode across the fields."

"How is he?" the Major asked, helping his wife to the ground.

"I haven't been in—been walking up and down out here. Thought I'd wait for you."

At the entrance of the passageway Louise met them. She kissed her mother, saying not a word. The Major held out his arms toward her. She pretended not to notice this complete surrender; she took his hand and turned her face from him.

"My poor little girl, I—"

She dropped his hand, opened the door of a room opposite

the dying man's chamber and said: "Step in here, please. Mother, you and Jim may come with me."

The old man broke down. "My precious child, God knows—"

"Will you please step in here? I will come with you. Mother, you and Jim—" She pointed to the door of her husband's room. In sorrowful obedience the Major bowed his head and crossed the threshold. In the room was a fire and on the mantel-piece a lamp was burning.

"Sit down," she said.

"Louise, I have not deserved this."

"Take the rocking chair, please."

He stood with his hands resting on the back of the chair. "Why do you hold me off with such stubbornness? Why continue to be so unnatural a child, so incomprehensible a woman?" Even now he did not forget to measure his sentences, but with the depth of his earnestness his voice was wavering, "You know—"

"Yes, I know," she broke in, looking full at him, and her face smote him with pity. "But this is no time for explanations." She turned toward the door.

"Are you going to leave me?" he asked, following her.

"Yes. Mother will tell you all that is to be told."

She went out and closed the door. The Major walked softly up and down the room, listening, but he heard nothing save the creaking of the house and the moaning of the wind in the old plum thicket. A long time passed, and then Mrs.

Cranceford entered. Her eyes were wet with tears. "It is all over," she said. At the moment the Major made no reply. He led her to a chair, and when she had sat down, looking up at him, he leaned over her and said: "Margaret, I know you can't help appreciating my position; and I feel that I am the keenest sufferer under this roof, for to me all consolation is denied. Now, what is expected of me? I am going to make no more protests—I am going to do as I am instructed. What is expected of me?"

"Go home, dear, and wait until I come," she answered.

"But doesn't that seem hard, Margaret?"

"Yes; but it is her wish and we must not oppose it."

"I will do as you say," he replied, and kissing her he added: "If you can, make her feel that I love her. Tell her that I acknowledge all the wrong." He stepped out into the passage, but he came back to the door, and standing there for a moment, he said: "Make her feel that I love her."

CHAPTER XIII

Pennington was buried in the yard of the church wherein he had taught school. No detail of the arrangements was submitted to the Major. For a time he held out that the family burial ground was the proper place for the interment, under the trees where his father and his mother were laid to rest, but Louise stood in strong opposition to this plan, even though appearances called for its adoption. So, after this, the Major offered no suggestion.

At the grave there was no hysterical grief. The day was bleak and the services were short. When all had been done, the Major gently put his arm about his daughter and said that she must go home with him.

"Not now," she replied; and she did not look up at him. "But please don't worry over me; don't feel that you have to do something. Mother is going with me, and after that you may know what I intend to do. Please don't urge me. Let me have my way just a little longer."

He stepped back from her and Mrs. Cranceford took her arm and led her away. The Major slowly followed them. He felt the inquisitive look of a neighbor, and his shoulders stiffened.

In a buggy the mother and the daughter had followed the hearse; the Major, Tom and big Jim Taylor were driven in the family carriage. Louise was to go back to the desolate house. The Major stoutly opposed this, pleaded with her after she had seated herself in the buggy, clutched the spoke of a muddy wheel as if he would hold her back. She took the lines from her mother, tossed them upon the horse, folded her arms, and in silence waited.

"John, dear," said Mrs. Cranceford, "let us drive on. There, please don't attract the attention of those people. You know what gossips they are."

The Major spoke to Louise. "Will you answer me one question?"

"Yes, sir."

"Is it your intention to live alone in that wretched house?"

"No, sir; but I must go there to think."

The Major stepped back, and with a handkerchief wiped his muddy hand. "Margaret, I leave her with you," he said.

Shortly after the Major reached home his wife arrived, but Louise was not with her. "I could do nothing," she said. "When we drove up to the gate she jumped out and declared that I must come on home. I pleaded with her, but she wouldn't yield. Two old women were in the house and she said that they were company enough; she wanted to think and they would not distract her thoughts. I told her that if she would agree to let me stay I would not say a word, but she shook her head. 'You shall hear from me to-morrow,' were her words, 'but you must leave me to myself to-night. It is of no use to urge me.' I saw that it wasn't, and I drove away. I declare I can't make her out."

"Most unreasonable creature I ever saw," the Major replied, uneasily walking up and down the room. "She has made me contemptible in the eyes of this neighborhood, and now appears determined to disgrace herself."

"Don't say that, John."

"Why not? It's a fact."

"It is not a fact. I am not afraid of a daughter of mine disgracing herself. It's only bad blood that disgraces itself."

"I am not so sure about that when women throughout the entire country are striving to be unnatural. By the blood—"

"John."

He wheeled about and looked at her. "But I ask you if it isn't enough to make a saint pull out his hair? Simply opposed her marriage, used legitimate argument, and afterward begged like a dog. Isn't it enough to make me spurn the restraints of the church and take up the language of the mud-clerk?"

"No, dear; nothing should prompt you to do that. You have a soul to be saved."

"But is it necessary that my life should be tortured out of me in order that my soul may be saved? I don't care to pay such a price. Is it put down that I must be a second Job? Is a boil the sign of salvation?"

"For goodness' sake don't talk that way," she pleaded, but she had to turn her face away to hide her smile from him.

"But I've got to talk some way. Just reflect on her treatment of me and how I have humbled myself and whined at her feet. And I ask what may we not expect of such a creature? Is it that she wants to be different from anyone else? Let me tell you one thing: The woman who seeks to be strongly individualized may attain her aim, but it leads to a sacrifice of her modesty. I say she is in danger of disgracing herself."

Mrs. Cranceford shook her head. "You wait and we shall see. No member of my family was ever disgraced. I may be distressed at her peculiarities, at times, but I shall never be afraid for her conduct."

Early the next morning a negro brought a letter from Louise. Mrs. Cranceford hastened to the office to read it to the Major. It appeared to have been written with care and thus was it worded:

"My Dear Mother:—I am thankful that I am not to look upon the surprise and sorrow you must feel in reading this letter. I hardly know how to rake together and assort what I desire to say, but I will do the best I can, and if you fail to understand me, do not charge it against yourself, but list it with my other faults. What I have recently gone through with is quite enough to unstring the nerves of a stronger woman than I am, and what must be my condition? Worn out and weary of any life that I could conceive of here—don't you see how I am floundering about? But give me time and in all honesty you shall know the true state of my mind. Many a time father has said that he did not understand me, and more than once you have charged me with being strange. But I am sure that I have never tried to be mysterious. I have had thoughts that would not have appeared sane, had I written them, but I have never been foolishly romantic, although my education has been far from practical. The first thing I remember was a disappointment, and that was not being a boy. It may be a vanity, but at that early age I seemed to recognize the little privileges given to a boy and denied a girl. But as I grew older I was shocked by the roughness and cruelty of boys, and then I was pleased to reflect that I was of gentler mold. At some time of life I suppose we are all enigmas unto ourselves; the mystery of being, the ability to move, and the marvelous something we call emotion, startles us and drives us into a moody and speculative silence. I give this in explanation of my earlier strangeness. I could always talk readily, but never, not even to you, could I tell completely what I thought. Most young people are warned against the trash that finds its way—no one appears to know how—into the library of the home, but I remember to have been taken to task for reading mannish books. And in some measure I heeded the lecture thus delivered, but it is to mannish books that I owe my semblance of common sense."

"What is she trying to get at?" the Major broke in. "Have you read it? If you have, tell me what she says."

"I am reading it now," his wife replied; and thus she continued:

"The strongest emotion of my life has been pity, and you know that I never could keep a doll nor a trinket if a strong appeal was made for it. I grew up to know that this was a weakness rather than a virtue, but never has my judgment been strong enough to prevail against it. And this leads me to speak of my marriage. That was the result of pity and fear. Let me see if I can make you understand me. That poor man's condition smote my heart as never before had it been smitten. And when he made his appeal to me, hollowed-eyed and coughing, I trembled, for I knew that my nature would prompt me to yield, although I might fully estimate the injustice to myself. So my judgment fought with my sense of pity, and in the end, perhaps, might have conquered it, but for the element of fear which was then introduced. The question of his soul was brought forward, and he swore that I would send it to heaven or to hell. In the light of what I have read, and in the recollection of what I have often heard father say in his arguments with preachers, perhaps I should have been strong enough to scout the idea of a literal torment, but I could not. You remember old Aunt Betsy Taylor, Jim's black mammy. When I was very young she was still living on the place, and was to me a curiosity, the last of her race, I was told. I did not know what this meant, but it gave her words great weight. Once she pictured hell for me, the roaring furnace, the writhing of the damned, and no reason and no reading has ever served to clear my mind of her awful painting. With her as the advocate I could hear the groans of lost souls; and in my childish way I believed that the old woman was inspired to spread the terrors of perdition; nor has education and the little I have seen of society, wholly changed this belief. So when Mr. Pennington swore to me that if I refused to marry him he would die blaspheming the name of God, my judgment tottered and fell. I sit here now, looking at the bed whereon he died. You saw him breathe his last, saw his smile of peace and hope. That smile was my reward. For it I had wrung the heart of my father and wiped my feet upon his pride. But I had sent a soul above. I have set myself to the task of perfect frankness, and I must tell you that in my heart there was not the semblance of love for him, love as you know it; there was only pity and I can say that pity is not akin to love. Yes. I sold myself, not as many a woman has, not as I would have been praised and flattered for doing—not for money, but to save a soul. This is written at night, with a still clock above me, the hands recording the hour and the minute of his death, and the light of the sun may fade my words and make them ghastly, but I am revealing, to my mother, my inner self."

Mrs. Cranceford paused to wipe her eyes, and the Major,

who had been walking up and down the room, now stood looking through the window at the sweep of yellow river, far away.

"But does she say when she is coming home?" he asked without turning his head. "Read on, please."

The sheets were disarranged and it was some time before she obeyed. "Read on, please," he repeated, and he moved from the window and stood with his hands resting on the back of a chair. Mrs. Cranceford read on:

"There is one misfortune of mine that has always been apparent to you and that is my painful sensitiveness. It was, however, not looked upon as a misfortune, but rather as a fault which at will I might correct, but I could no more have obviated it than I could have changed my entire nature. When father charged me with ingratitude I realized the justice of the rebuke (from his point of view), while feeling on my side the injustice of the imputation, for I was not ungrateful, but simply in a desperate state of mind. I am afraid that I am not making myself clear. But let me affirm that I do not lose sight of the debt I owe him, the debt of gallantry. I had always admired him for his bravery, and hundreds of times have I foolishly day-dreamed of performing a life-saving office for him. But the manner—and pardon me for saying it—the arrogance which he assumed over me, wounded me, and the wound is still slowly bleeding. But in time it will heal, and when it does I will go to him, but now I cannot."

"But she must come to me or let me go to her!" the Major broke in. "I confess that I didn't understand her. Why, there is heroism in her composition. Go ahead, Margaret. She's got more sense than all of us. Go ahead."

Mrs. Cranceford continued: "I can conceive of nothing more useless than my life at home would be. The truth is, I must do something, see something, feel the throb rather than the continuous pressure of life. Thousands of women are making their way in the world. Why should not I? And it is not that I mean wholly to desert you or to love you less, but I must go away, and before this letter reaches you I shall be on my journey—"

Mrs. Cranceford's trembling hands let the paper fall. The Major grabbed it up, fumbled with it, put it upon the desk and sat down. In silence they looked at each other, and their vision was not clear. "Read on," he said. "We can stand anything now."

She wiped her eyes and obeyed him: "Shall be on my journey. I have in mind a certain place, but what place it is I must not tell you. If I succeed I shall let you know, and if I fail—but I will base nothing upon the probability of failure. I know that you will look upon this almost as an act of insanity, and carrying out my resolve to be frank, I must say that I do not know but that it is. It is, though, the only course that promises relief and therefore I must take it. You must not charge me with a lack of love for you and never must you lose faith in me. It is singular that after all these years, after all our confidences, I should choose a pen wherewith to make myself known to you, and you may call me a most unnatural daughter, but you must charge my unnaturalness to nature, and nothing that nature does should appear unnatural when once we have come to understand it. I have money enough to last me until I can secure employment. I hope that I know what sort of employment it may be, but as there is in my hope a fear of failure, I will not tell you. My training has not been systematic enough to enable me to be a school teacher, for I know a little of many things, but am thorough in nothing. But in some other line the mannish books may help me. In reading this over I realize that I am vain and affected. But put it down as another frankness. God bless you and good-bye."

"I told you she would disgrace herself," the Major exclaimed, slapping his hand upon the desk.

"She has done nothing of the sort," his wife replied, stepping out and closing the door.

CHAPTER XIV

The neighbors were curious to know why Louise had left home and whither she was gone. Day and night they came to ask questions, and though told that she was visiting relatives in Kentucky, they departed suspecting that something must be wrong. The gossips were more or less busy, and Jim Taylor snatched another idler off the fence and trounced him in the sand.

Weeks passed and no letter came from Louise. The Major worried over her until at last he forbade the mention of her name. During the day Mrs. Cranceford was calm and brave, but many a time in the night the Major heard her crying. Every Sunday afternoon Jim Taylor's tread was heard on the porch. To the Major he talked of various things, of the cotton which was nearly all picked, of the weakening or strengthening tendency of the market, but when alone with Mrs. Cranceford his talk began and ended with Louise. But in this he observed the necessity for great care, lest the Major might hear him, and he chose occasions when the old gentleman was in his office or when with Gid he strolled down into the woods. In the broad parlor, in the log part of the house, Jim and Mrs. Cranceford would sit, hours at a time; and never did she show an impatience of his long lapses of silence nor of his monotonous professions of faith in the run-away. And upon taking his leave he would never fail to say: "I believe we'll hear from her to-morrow; I am quite sure of it."

In the midst of the worry that followed the young woman's departure, there had been but one mention of the young man's affair with the niece of Wash Sanders. Mrs. Cranceford had spoken to him, not directly, but with gentle allusion, and he had replied with an angry denunciation of such meddlesomeness. "I'm not going to marry a dying woman," he declared; "and I'm not going to take up any faded ninny that you and father may pick out. I'm going to please myself, and when you decide that I mustn't, just say the word and I'll hull out. And I don't want to hear anything about crackers or white trash, either. That's me."

His mother must have agreed that it was, for the weeks went by and not again did she drop a hint of her anxiety.

One rainy afternoon the Major and old Gid were sitting on a tool-box under the barn shed, when Father Brennon came riding down the road.

"As they say over the creek, light and look at your saddle!" the Major shouted.

With a nod and a smile the priest rode through the gate, dismounted, gave his horse over to a negro who, in answer to a shout, had come forward from some mysterious precinct of the barn-yard, shook hands with the Major and Gid, and gracefully declining a seat on the tool-box, rolled a barrel from against the wall and upon it seated himself.

"More in accordance with the life of a priest," he said, tapping the barrel with his knuckles. "It is rolling."

"Ah," replied the Major, "and a barrel may also typify the

reckless layman. It is often full."

The priest gave to this remark the approval of a courteous laugh. Even though he might stand in a slippery place, how well he knew his ground. To call forth a weak joke and then to commend it with his merriment—how delightful a piece of flattery. And it can, in truth, be said that in his heart he was sincere. To be pleasing was to him an art, and this art was his second nature.

"Mr. Brennon," said the Major (and under no compulsion would he have said father), "I have thought a great deal of the argument we had some time ago; and I have wondered, sir, that in coming to this community to proselyte the negro, you did not observe the secrecy with which the affairs of your church are usually conducted. But understand, please, that I do not mean to reflect upon the methods of your creed, but simply wonder that you have not followed a recognized precedent."

The priest had taken hold of the chine at each end of the barrel and was slowly rolling himself backward and forward. "I fail to see why any secrecy should be observed in my work," he replied. "The Catholic church has never made a secret of doing good—for we believe in the potency of example. If we elevate the moral condition of one man, it is well that another man should know it. The Methodist holds his revival and implores the sinner to come forward and kneel at the altar. And as it were, I am holding a revival—I am persuading the negro and the white man as well to kneel under the cross. Should there be any secrecy in such a work?"

"Well, no, not when you put it that way. But you know that we look upon the Catholic religion as a foreign religion. It does not somehow seem native to this soil. It is red with the pomp of monarchy, it has the ceremonious restraint of the king's court; it hasn't the free noise of a republic. I will not question its sincerity or the fact that it has in view the betterment of man, but to us it will always seem an importation."

"It was here first," the priest replied, gravely smiling. "It discovered this country."

"We must grant that," the Major rejoined, "but still I insist that the native born American regards it as a foreign institution, foreign to his nature, to his sense of liberty, if not to his soul."

"My dear Major, Christ is foreign to no soil. The earth is His Father's foot-stool. The soul of man is the abiding place of the love of the Saviour, and no heart is out-landish. What you may call liberty is an education, but the soul as God's province is not made so by training, but came with the first twinkling of light, of reason, the dawn of time."

"That's about as straight as any man can give it," old Gid joined in. "But what puzzles me is why God is more at home in one man's heart than in another. He fills some hearts with love and denies it to others; and the heart that has been denied is cursed, through no fault of its own—simply because it has not received—while the other heart is blessed. I reckon the safest plan is to conclude that we don't know anything about it. I don't, and that settles it so far as I'm concerned. I can't accept man's opinion, for man doesn't know any more about it than I do; so I say to myself, 'Gideon Batts, eat, drink and be merry, for the first thing you know they will come along and lay you out where the worm is whetting his appetite.' You have raked up quite a passle of negroes, haven't you, colonel?"

The priest looked at him, but not resentfully. "My work has

not been without a fair measure of success," he answered, now sitting upright and motionless. "You must have noticed that we are building quite a large church."

"So I see," said the Major. "And you still believe that you are going to preserve the negro's body as well as save his soul."

"We are going to save his soul, and a soul that is to be saved serves to protect its habitation."

"But you foresee a race war?"

"I foresee racial troubles, which in time may result in a war of extermination."

"I agree with you, Mr. Brennon," the Major replied. "As time passes it will become more and more clear that the whites and the negroes cannot live together. Their interests may be identical, but they are of a different order and can never agree. And now let us face the truth. What sowed the seeds of this coming strife? Emancipation? No, enfranchisement. The other day Mr. Low gave me a copy of the London Spectator, calling my attention to a thoughtful paper on this very subject. It deeply impressed me, so much so that I read parts of it a number of times. Let me see if I can recall one observation that struck me. Yes, and it is this: 'We want a principle on which republicans can work and we believe that the one which would be the most fruitful is that the black people should be declared to be foreign immigrants, guests of the state, entitled to the benefit of every law and every privilege, education, for example, but debarred from political power and from sitting on juries, which latter, indeed, in mixed cases, ought to be superseded by properly qualified magistrates and judges.' The paper goes on to show that this would not be oppressive, and that the blacks would be in the position of a majority of Englishmen prior to 1832, a position compatible with much happiness. But the trouble is we have gone too far to retrace our steps. It was easy enough to grant suffrage to the negro, but to take it away would be a difficult matter. So what are we to do? To let the negro exercise the full and unrestrained measure of his suffrage, would, in some communities, reduce the white man to the position of political nonentity. And no law, no cry about the rights of a down-trodden race, no sentiment expressed abroad, could force the white man to submit quietly to this degradation. Upon the negro's head the poetry of New England has placed a wreath of sentiment. No poet has placed a wreath upon the brow of the California Chinaman, nor upon the head of any foreign element in any of the northern states. Then why this partiality? Is the negro so gentle that he must always be defended, and is the white man of the south so hard of heart that he must always be condemned?"

"What you say is perfectly clear to me," the priest replied, "and it is natural that you should defend your position."

"It is the only position and the only course left to a thinking and a self-respecting white man," the Major rejoined.

"Yes, I will agree to that, too."

"Ah, and that's the trouble, Mr. Brennon. You agree while you oppose."

"My dear Major, I am not here to oppose, nor to destroy, but to save fragments when the hour of destruction shall have come."

"But if your church believes that it can save fragments why doesn't it exert itself to save the whole?"

"Major, salvation comes of persuasion and persuasion is slow."

"Yes, and let me tell you that your form of religion will never become popular among the negroes. The negro is emotional, and to make a display of his religious agitation is too great a luxury to be given up. Your creed entails too much belief and too little excitement; upon the layman it doesn't confer sufficient importance. The negro must shout and hug. The quiet mysticism of the divine spirit does not satisfy him. He wants to be exorcised; he wants what is known as the mourners'-bench jerks. If his brother loves him he doesn't want a quiet assurance of that fact, conveyed by a year of conduct; he demands a noisy proof, the impulse of a moment of joy."

With a slow shake of his head old Gid confirmed this view, and the priest looked on, gravely smiling. "You have now touched upon a mistaken phase of the negro's character," said he. "And to make my point clear, I must speak plainly with regard to the appearance of our form of worship. I must present it as it impresses the ignorant and the superstitious. In doing so I make myself appear almost irreverent, but in no other way can I show you the possibilities of my work among the colored race. Mystery appeals to the negro. Behind all mystery there is power. Under the influence of the sensationalist the negro may shout, demand an impulsive proof of love, hug his brother; but in his heart God is a fearful and silent mystery. And the Catholic church shows him that the holy spirit is without noise. In the creation of the great tree there has not been a sound; all has been the noiseless will of God. It is not difficult to show him that ours was the first church; it may be shown that the Protestant Bible held him a slave; and above all we prove to him that in the Catholic church there is no discrimination against his color, that a negro may become a Cardinal. We convince him that shouting is but a mental agitation and a physical excitement. I have know many a negro, on the scaffold, to renounce the religion which for years he had practiced, and with cool discernment embrace the parent church. The germ of Catholicism is in his blood. He cannot be a free thinker. The barbarian is subdued by the solemn and majestic form of the Church of Rome, while he might regard with disdain the intricate reason of the Presbyterian faith. And in this respect the negro is akin to the barbarian. He is moved by music and impressed by ceremony."

"You are plain-spoken, indeed," the Major replied. "The boldness with which you recount your shams is most surprising. I didn't expect it."

"I told you that I would be bold."

"But you didn't say that you would acknowledge your insincerity."

"Nor have I done so. I have simply shown you why our church appeals to the superstitious blood of the African. To accomplish a good we must use the directest means. If I were seeking to convert you, I should adopt a different method. I would appeal to your reason; convince you of a truth which the wisest men have known and still know—that the Catholic church is God's church. It is now time for me to go," he added, after a short pause. "Please tell your man that I want my horse."

CHAPTER XV

At the close of a misty day Jim Taylor stood at the parlor door to take his leave of Mrs. Cranceford. During the slow hours of the afternoon they had talked about Louise, or sitting in silence had thought of her; and now at parting there was nothing to be added except the giant's hopeful remark, "I believe we'll hear from her to-morrow; I am quite sure of it." Repetition may make a sentiment trite, and into a slangish phrase may turn a wise truism, but words spoken to encourage an anxious heart do not lose their freshness. "Yes, I am quite sure of it," he repeated. And the next day a letter came. It bore no post mark; the captain of a steamboat had sent it over from a wood-yard. The boat was an unimportant craft and its name was new even to the negroes at the landing, which, indeed, must have argued that the vessel was making its first trip on the Arkansas. The communication was brief, but it was filled with expressions of love. "I am beginning to make my way," the writer said, "and when I feel that I have completely succeeded, I will come home. My ambition now is to surprise you, and to do this I must keep myself in the dark just a little longer. I have tried to imagine myself a friendless woman, such as I have often read about, and I rather enjoy it. Love to Jim."

The Major was in his office when the letter was brought, and thither his wife hastened to read it to him.

"What is it?" he asked as she entered the room. "A letter from Louise? I don't want to hear it."

"John."

"I don't want to hear another crazy screed from her. Where is she? Is she coming home? Read it."

During the reading he listened with one hand cupped behind his ear—though his hearing was not impaired—and when the last word had been pronounced, he said: "Likes to be mysterious, doesn't she? Well, I hope she'll get enough of it. If her life has been so much influenced by sympathy why has she felt none of that noble quality for us? Where is she?"

"The letter doesn't say. It is not even dated, and it is not post-marked."

"Did it come in a gale? Was it blown out of a mysterious cloud?"

"It came from the wood-yard, and the man who brought it said that it had been left by the captain of the Mill-Boy, a new boat, they say."

"Well, it's devilish—"

"John."

"I say it's very strange. Enjoys being mysterious. I wonder if she equally enjoys having the neighbors talk about her? Sends love to Jim. Well, that isn't so bad. You'd better have some one take the letter over to him."

"I sent him word by the man who brought the letter that we had heard from her."

No further did the Major question her, but taking up a handful of accounts, he settled himself into the preoccupation in which she had found him, but the moment she went out and closed the door, he got out of his chair and with his hands behind him, walked up and down the room. At the window he halted, and standing there, looked down the river, in the direction of the cape of sand whereon Louise had stood, that day when Pennington coughed in the library door; and in his mind the old man saw her, with her hands clasped over her brown head. He mused over the time that had passed since then, the marriage, the death, the dreary funeral; and though he did not reproach himself, yet he felt that could he but recall that day he would omit his foolish plea of gallantry.

For the coming of Jim, Mrs. Cranceford had not long to wait. She was in the parlor when he tapped at the door. After she had called, "Come in," he continued to stand there as if he were afraid of meeting a disappointment. But when he had peeped in and caught sight of her smiling face, his cold fear was melted.

"Here it is," she said, holding the letter out to him. Almost at one stride he crossed the room and seized the letter. In the light of the window he stood to read it, but it fluttered away from him the moment he saw that there was a greeting in it for himself. He grabbed at it as if, possessing life, it were trying to escape, and with a tight grip upon it he said: "I knew she would write and I am sure she would have written sooner if—if it had been necessary."

Mrs. Cranceford was laughing tearfully. "Oh, you simple-hearted man, so trustful and so big of soul, what is your love not worth to a woman?"

"Simple-hearted? I am nothing of the sort. I try to be just and that's all there is to it."

"No, Jim Taylor, there's more to it than that. A man may be just and his sense of justice may demand a stricter accounting than you ask for."

"I guess you mean that I'm weak."

"Oh, no," she hastened to reply, "I don't mean that. The truth is I mean that you give something that but few men have ever given—a love blind enough and great enough to pardon a misdeed committed against yourself. It is a rare charity."

He did not reply, but in the light of the window he stood, reading the letter; and Mrs. Cranceford, sitting down, gave him the attention of a motherly fondness, smiling upon him; and he, looking up from the letter which a pleasurable excitement caused to shake in his hand, wondered why any one should ever have charged this kindly matron with a cold lack of sympathy. So interested in his affairs was she, so responsive to a sentiment, though it might be clumsily spoken, so patient of his talk and of his silence, that to him she was the Roman mother whom he had met in making his way through a short-cut of Latin.

"Jim."

"Yes, ma'm."

"I want to ask you something. Have you talked much with Tom lately?"

"Not a great deal. He was over at my place the other night and we talked of first one thing and then another, but I don't remember much of what was said. Why do you want to know?"

"Can't you guess?"

"Don't know that I can. I was always rather slow at guessing. And don't let me try; tell me what you mean?"

"You are as stupid as you are noble."

"What did you say, ma'm?" Again he had given his attention to the letter.

"Oh, nothing."

"But you must have said something," he replied, pressing the letter into narrow folds, and appearing as if he felt that he had committed a crime in having failed to catch the meaning of her remark.

"Oh, it amounted to nothing."

He stupidly accepted this decree, and smoothing out the letter and folding it again, requested that he might be permitted to take it home; and with this reply she gladdened him: "I intended that you should."

At evening old Gid came, with many a snort and many a noisy stamp at the dogs prancing upon the porch. Into the library he bustled, puffing and important, brisk with the air of business. "John," he said, as he sat down, "the last bale of my cotton has been hauled to the landing. It will be loaded to-night and to-morrow morning I'm going with it down to New Orleans; and I gad, I'll demand the last possible cent, for it's the finest staple I ever saw."

"I thought you were going to bunch in and sell with me," the Major replied.

"I intended to, John, but you see I'm too far ahead of you to wait. I don't like to discount my industry by waiting. The truth is, I want the money as soon as I can get it. I am chafing to discharge my debts. It may be noble to feel and acknowledge the obligations of friendship, but the consciousness of being in debt, a monied debt, even to a friend, is blunting to the higher sensibilities and hampering to the character. Now, you've never been in debt, and therefore you don't know what slavery is."

"What! I've owed fifty thousand dollars at a time."

"Yes, but you had a way of getting out from under it, John. We don't deserve any credit for paying a debt if it comes easy, if it's natural to us. Why, a man with the faculty of getting out from under a debt is better off and is more to be envied than the man who has never known what it is to walk under a weight of obligations, for to throw off the burden brings him a day of real happiness, while the more prudent and prosperous person is acquainted merely with contentment. You've had a good time in your life, John. On many an occasion when other men would have been at the end of the string you have reached back, grabbed up your resources and enjoyed them. Yes, sir. And you have more education than I have, but you can never hope to rival me in wisdom."

The Major was standing on the hearth, and leaning his head back against the mantel-piece, he laughed; and from Mrs. Cranceford's part of the house came the impatient slam of a door.

"It's a fact, John. And within me there is just enough of rascality to sweeten my wisdom."

"There is no doubt as to the rascality, Gid. The only question is with regard to the wisdom."

"Easy, John. The wisdom is sometimes hidden; modesty covers it up, and if the rascality is always apparent it is my frankness that holds it up to view. Yes, sir. But my wisdom lacks something, is in want of something to direct it. Pure wisdom can't direct itself, John; it is like gold—it must have an alloy. You've got that alloy, and it makes you more successful as a man, but sometimes less charming as a companion. The part of a man that means business is disagreeable to a gentle, humor-loving nature like mine. I perceive that I've got my speculative gear on, and I'm bold; yes, for I am soon to discharge a sacred obligation and then to walk out under the trees a free man. But I'm naturally bold. Did you ever notice that a sort of self-education makes a man adventurous in his talk when a more systematic training might hold him down with the clamps of too much care?"

"Yes, might inflict him with the dullness of precision," the Major suggested, smiling upon his guest.

"That's it, and for this reason half-educated men are often the brightest. I read a book—and I reckon I'm as fond of a good book as any man—without bringing to bear any criticisms that scholars have passed upon it. But with you it is different."

"Gid, you ascribe scholarship to me when in fact you are far more bookish than I am. You sit in your den all alone and read while I'm shut up in my office going over my accounts. From care you have a freedom that I can never hope to find."

"John, in comparison with me you don't know what care is."

The Major leaned against the mantel-piece and laughed.

"It's a fact, John. Why, I have care enough to kill a statesman or strain a philosopher. Look at me; I'm old and don't amount to anything, and that is one of the heaviest cares that can settle down upon man. Wise? Oh, yes, we'll grant that, but as I before remarked, my wisdom lacks proper direction. It is like ill-directed energy, and that, you know, counts for nothing. I once knew a fellow that expended enough energy in epileptic fits to have made him a fortune. He'd fall down and kick and paw the air—a regular engine of industry, but it was all wasted. But he had a brother, a lazy fellow, and he conceived the idea of a sort of gear for him, so that his jerkings and kicks operated a patent churn. So, if I only had some ingenious fool to harness me I might do something."

"Why," said the Major, "I wouldn't have you otherwise than what you are. Suppose you were to become what might be termed a useful citizen, truthful and frugal—"

"Hold on, John," Gid broke in, holding up his hands. "You distress me with your picture. When I hear of a frugal man I always imagine he's hungry. Yes, sir. But let me tell you, I'll be a man of affairs when I come back from New Orleans. You may be assured of that. I'm going to scatter money about this neighborhood. Why, every lout within ten miles square, if he's got fifteen dollars, holds his opinion above mine. Ah, by a lucky chance I see that your demijohn is in here. And now just fill up this bottle," he added, producing a flask as if by a sleight-of-hand trick, "and I will bid you good-night."

CHAPTER XVI

A neighboring planter, having just returned from New Orleans, told the Major that in the French market he had met Gid, who had informed him that for his cotton he had received a premium above the highest price, in recognition of its length of fibre and the care with which it had been handled. The part of the statement that bore upon the length of fibre was accepted by the Major, but he laughed at the idea that Gid's care should call for reward. But so good a report was pleasing to him and he told his wife that her denunciation of the old fellow must soon be turned into praise. And with cool thoughtfulness she thus replied: "John, is it possible that at this late day you are still permitting that man to fill your eyes with dust? Has he again wheedled you into the belief that he is going to pay you? It does seem to me that your good sense ought to show you that man as he really is."

They were at the dinner table. The Major shoved back his chair and looked at his wife long and steadily. "Margaret," said he, "there is such a thing as persecution, and you are threatened with a practice of it. But do I believe he is going to pay me? I do. And naturally you want to know my reason for thinking so."

"Yes, I should like to know. I suppose your kindness rather

than your judgment has found a reason. It always does."

"Good; and the reason which a kindness discovers, though the search for it may be a mistake, is better than the spirit that inspires a persecution. However, we won't indulge in any fine-drawn argument; we will—"

"Search for another reason when one is exploded," she suggested, victoriously smiling upon him.

"Oh, you mean that I really haven't found one. To tell you the truth I haven't a very strong one. But in some way he has convinced me of his sincerity. I have forced upon him the understanding that at least a good part of the money must be paid, and the fact that he took me seriously, forms, perhaps, the basis of my belief in his desire to face his obligations. We shall see."

Several days passed, but they saw nothing of Gid. It was known that he was at home, for Jim Taylor had told the news of his return. At this neglect the Major was fretted, and one morning he sent word to Gid that he must come at once and give an account of himself. It was nearly noon when the old fellow arrived. Clumsily he dismounted from his horse, and meekly he made his way into the yard, tottering as he walked. He appeared to have lost flesh, and his skin was yellow with worry and with want of sleep. The Major came forward and they met and shook hands under a tree. From an upper window Mrs. Cranceford looked upon them.

"Gid, I didn't know what had become of you. I heard of you after you had received for your cotton more than the market price, and—"

"It was a fine shipment, John. Have you a rope handy? I want to hang myself. And why? Because I don't expect anyone to believe my statement; but John, as sure as I am alive this minute, my pocket was picked in the French market. Hold on, now. I don't ask you to believe me, for I won't be unreasonable, but I hope I may drop dead this moment if I wasn't robbed. And that's the reason I have held back. Get the rope and I'll hang myself. I don't want to live any longer. I am no account on the face of the earth. I sang like a cricket when I might have been more in earnest, and now when my condition is desperate, the fact that I have been foolish and careless takes all weight from my words. As I came along my old horse stumbled, and I didn't try to check him—I wanted him to fall and kill me. Get me the rope."

The Major took off his hat and leaned against the tree. With humility, with drooping patience, Gid waited for him to speak, and his ear was strained to catch the familiar word of hope, or mayhap the first bar of a resounding laugh. The first words escaped him; he heard only their cold tone without comprehending their meaning:

"I want you to get off that place just as soon as you can; and I want you to go as you came—with nothing. I have laughed at you while you were cheating me; I have placed a premium upon your worthlessness and rascality. There is no good in you. Get off that place just as soon as you can."

"John—"

"Don't call me John. You are a hypocrite and a deadbeat. Yes, you have sung like a cricket and I have paid dearly for your music. Don't say a word to me; don't open your lying mouth, but get out of this yard as soon as your wretched legs can carry you, and get off that place at once."

The Major turned his back upon him, and the old fellow tottered to the gate. With an effort he scrambled upon his horse and was gone. He looked back as if he expected to see a hand upraised, commanding him to stop; he listened for a voice inviting him to return; but he saw no hand, heard no voice, and onward down the road he went. In the highway he met a man and the man spoke to him, but he replied not, neither did he lift his heavy eyes, but rode onward, drooping over the horse's neck. He passed the house of Wash Sanders, and from the porch the invalid hailed him, but he paid no heed.

Upon reaching home, or the cypress log house which for him had so long been a free and easy asylum, he feebly called a negro to take his horse. Into the house he went, into the only habitable room. It was at best a desolate abode; the walls were bare, the floor was rotting, but about him he cast a look of helpless affection, at the bed, at a shelf whereon a few books were piled. He opened a closet and took therefrom a faded carpet-bag and into it he put Rousseau's Confessions, then an old book on logic, and then he hesitated and looked up at the shelf. All were dear to him, these thumbed and dingy books; many a time at midnight had they supped with him beside the fire of muttering white-oak coals, and out into the wild bluster of a storm had they driven care and loneliness. But he could not take them all. Painfully he made his selections, nearly filled his bag, leaving barely room for an old satin waistcoat and two shirts; and these he stuffed in hastily. He put the bag upon the bed, when with fumbling he had fastened it, and stood looking about the room. Yes, that was all, all except a hickory walking cane standing in a corner.

Onward again he went with his cane on his shoulder and his bag on his back. At the bars down the lane a dog ran up to him. "Go to the house, Jack," he said, and the dog understood him and trotted away, but in the old man's voice he heard a suspicious note and he turned before reaching the house and followed slowly and cautiously, stopping whenever the old fellow turned to look back. At the corner of a field Gid halted and put down his bag, and the dog turned about, pretending to be on his way home. In the field was a pecan tree, tall and graceful. Year after year had the old man tended it, and to him it was more than a tree, it was a friend. Upon the fence he climbed, sitting for a moment on the top rail to look about him; to the tree he went, and putting his arms about it, pressed his wrinkled cheek against its bark. He turned away, climbed the fence, took up his bag and resumed his journey toward the steamboat landing. Far behind, on a rise in the road, the dog sat, watching him. The old man turned a bend in the road, and the dog, running until his master was again in sight, sat down to gaze after him. Far ahead was the charred skeleton of a gin house, burned by marauders many years ago, and here he was to turn into the road that led to the landing. He looked up as he drew near and saw a horse standing beside the road; and then from behind the black ruin stepped a man—the Major.

"Gid," he said, coming forward, "I believe we're going to have more rain."

The old man dropped his bag, and the dog far down the road turned back. "Wind's from the northwest, Gid." He put his hand on the old fellow's shoulder.

"Don't touch me, John; let me go."

"Why, I can't let you go. Look here, old man, you have stood by me more than once—you stood when other men ran away—and you are more to me than money is."

"Let me go, John. I am an old liar and an old hypercrite. My pocket was not picked—I lost the money gambling. Let me go; I am a scoundrel."

He stooped to take up his bag, but the Major seized it. "I'll carry it for you," he said. "Too heavy for as old a man as you are. Come on back and raise another crop."

"I haven't a thing to go on, John. Can't even get feed for the mules. Give me the satchel."

"You shall have all the feed you want."

"But your wife—"

"I will tell her that the debt is paid."

"John, your gospel would take the taint out of a thief on a cross. And I was never so much of a man as you now make me, and, I gad, I'm going to be worthy of your friendship. Let me remind you of something: That old uncle of mine in Kentucky will leave me his money. It's cold-blooded to say it, but I understand that he can't live but a short time. I am his only relative, and have a hold on him that he can't very well shake off. He'll beat me out of my own as long as he can, but old Miz Nature's got her eye on him. Yes, I'll try it again and next year I'll let you sell the crop. But say, John, at one time I had them fellows on the hip, and if I had cashed in at the right time I would have hit 'em big. Get your horse and we'll hook the satchel over the horn of the saddle."

Along the road they walked toward home, the Major leading the horse. For a time they were silent, and then the Major said: "As I came along I was thinking of that bully from Natchez. He would have killed me with his Derringer if you hadn't broken his arm with your cane."

"Oh, yes; that red-headed fellow. It has been a long time since I thought of him. How the pleasant acquaintances of our younger days do slip away from us."

"Yes," the Major laughed, "and our friends fall back as we grow old. Friendship is more a matter of temperament than—"

"Of the honesty of the other party," Gid suggested.

"Yes, you are right. Honesty doesn't always inspire friendship, for we must be interested in a man before we can become his friend; and mere honesty is often a bore."

When they reached the gate that opened into Gid's yard, the Major shook hands with the old fellow and told him to resume his authority as if nothing had happened to interrupt it.

"I will, John; but something has happened to interrupt it, and that interruption has been my second birth, so to speak. I passed away at twelve o'clock and was born again just now. I won't try to express my feelings, I am still so young; for any profession of gratitude would be idle in comparison with what I am going to do. I've got your friendship and I'm going to have your respect. Come in and sit awhile, won't you?"

"Not now, but I'll come over to-night."

"Good. And remember this, John; I'm going to have your respect."

CHAPTER XVII

With a generous and perhaps weak falsehood the Major sought to assure his wife that Gid had paid a part of his debt, and that a complete settlement was not far off, but with a cool smile she looked at him and replied: "John, please don't tax your conscience any further. It's too great a strain on you. Let the matter drop. I won't even say I told you so."

"And as much as you might want the subject to be dropped you can't let it fall without reminding me—but we will let it drop; we'll throw it down. But you have your rights, Margaret, and they shall be respected. I will tell him that out of respect to you he must stay away from here."

"That is very thoughtful, dear; but does it occur to you that your continued intimacy with him, whether he comes here or not, will show a want of respect for me?"

"You don't give a snap whether he pays his debts or not. You simply don't want me to associate with him. No, it has not occurred to me that I am not showing you proper respect and neither is it true. Margaret, do you know what is the most absurd and insupportable tyranny that woman can put upon man? It is to choose a companion for her husband."

"With me, dear, it is not tyranny; it is judgment."

"Oh, yes; or rather, it is the wonderful intuition which we are taught to believe that woman possesses. I admit that she is quick to see evil in a man, but she shuts her eyes to the good quality that stands opposite to offset it."

"Oh, I know that I haven't shrewdness enough to discover a good trait; I can recognize only the bad, for they are always clearly in view. It is a wonder that you can respect so stupid a creature as I am, and I know that you have ceased to have a deeper feeling for me."

"Now, Margaret, for gracious sake don't talk that way. Oh, of course you've got me now, and I have to flop or be a brute. Yes, you've got me. You know I respect your good sense and love you, so what's the use of this wrangle. There, now, it's all right. I'll promise not to go near him if you say so. And I have made up my mind to attend church with more regularity. I acknowledge that I can go wrong oftener than almost any man. Respect for you!" he suddenly broke out. "Why, you are the smartest woman in this state, and everybody knows it. Come on out to the office and sit with me."

Sometimes the Major, with a pretense of having business to call him away at night, would go over to old Gid's house, and together they would chuckle by the fire or nod over roasting potatoes. They talked of their days on the river, and of their nights at Natchez under the hill. To be wholly respectable, a man must give up many an enjoyment, but when at last he has become virtuous, he fondly recounts the escapades of former years; and thus the memory of hot blood quickens the feeble pulse of age.

Sometimes old Gid would meet the Major at the gin house and joke with him amid the dust and lint, but he always came and departed in a roundabout way, so that Mrs. Cranceford, sitting at the window, might not be offended by his horse and his figure in the road. A time came when there was an interval of a week, and the old fellow had not shown himself at the gin house, and one night the Major went to the cypress log home to invade his retirement, but the place was dark. He pushed open the door and lighted the lamp. The fireplace was cheerless with cold ashes. He went to a cabin and made inquiry of a negro, and was told that Mr. Batts had been gone more than a week, and that he had left no word as to when he intended to return. Greatly worried, the Major went home; wide awake he pondered during long hours in bed, but no light fell upon the mystery of the old man's absence; nor in the night nor at breakfast did the Major speak of it to his wife, but silently he took his worry with him to his office. One morning while the planter was at his desk, there came a storming at the dogs in the yard.

"Get down, boys. Don't put your muddy paws on me. Hi, there, Bill, you seven years' itch of a scoundrel, take my horse to the stable."

The Major threw open the door. "Don't come out, John!" Gid shouted, coming forward among the prancing dogs. "Don't come out, for I want to see you in there."

He appeared to have gained flesh; his cheeks were ruddy, and his grasp was strong as he seized the Major's hand. "How are you, John?"

"Why, old man, where on earth have you been?"

"I have been in the swamp for many years, but now I touch the ground only in high places."

He boldly stepped into the office, and as he sat down the sweep of his coat-tails brushed chattel mortgages and bills of sale from the desk. "Only in high places do my feet touch the ground, John. I have just returned from Kentucky. And I bring the news that my old uncle is no more to this life, but is more to me than ever."

"And you were summoned to his bedside," said the Major, striving to be serious, but smiling upon him.

"Not exactly. You might say that I was summoned by a lawyer to his chest-side. He left me no word of affection, but his money is mine, and on many a half-dollar of it I warrant you there is the print of his tooth. Give me your check-book, John."

"Wait a while, Gid. Let us accustom ourselves to the situation."

"No; let us get down to business. I am impatient to pay a mildewed debt. God's love was slow, John, but it came. How much do I owe?"

"I don't believe I'd pay it all at once, Gid. Leave a part to be met by the next crop."

"All right; but it's yours at any time. The only way I can use money is to get rid of it as soon as possible. Make out a check for two-thirds of the amount and I'll put my strong hand to it. But you haven't congratulated me."

"No," the Major replied, with a drawl, "for I felt that it would have too much the appearance of my own greed. I have hounded you—" The old fellow seized him, and stopped his utterance. "Don't say that, John. You have kept me out of hell and you ought to complete my heaven with a congratulation."

They shook hands, looking not into each other's eyes, but

downward; the Major pretended to laugh, and old Gid, dropping his hand, blustered about the room, whistled and stormed at a dog that poked his head in at the door. Then he sat down, crossed his legs; but finding this uncomfortable, sprawled himself into an easier position and began to moralize upon the life and character of his uncle. "He always called me a fool with an uproarious fancy, an idiot with wit, and a wise man lacking in sense. He denied himself everything, and it strikes me that he must have been the fool. I wish he had gathered spoil enough to make me rich, but I reckon he did the best he could, and I forgive him. We must respect the dead, and sometimes the sooner they are dead the sooner we respect them. Let me sign that thing. Oh, he hasn't left me so much, but I won't quarrel with him now. What was it the moralist said?" he asked, pressing a blotting pad upon his name. "Said something about we must educate or we must perish. That's all right, but I say we must have money. Without money you may be honest," he went on, handing the check to the Major, "but your honesty doesn't show to advantage. Money makes a man appear honorable whether he is or not. It gives him courage, and nothing is more honorable than courage. The fact that a man pays a debt doesn't always argue that he's honest—it more often argues that he's got money. Accident may make a man honest just as it may make him a thief."

"Your log fire and your old books haven't done you any harm, Gid."

"They have saved my life, John. And let me tell you, that a man who grows gray without loving some old book is worse than a fool. The quaint thought of an old thinker is a cordial to aged men who come after him. I used to regret that I had not been better educated, but now I'm glad that my learning is not broader—it might give me too many loves—might make me a book polygamist. I have wondered why any university man can't sit down and write a thing to startle the world; but the old world herself is learned, and what she demands is originality. We may learn how to express thought, John, but after all, thought itself must be born in us. There, I have discharged an obligation and delivered a moral lecture, and I want to tell you that you are the best man I ever saw."

"Now you are talking nonsense, Gid. Why, you have been just as necessary to me as I have to you. In a manner you have been the completion of myself."

"Ah," Gid cried, scuffling to his feet and bowing, "I have the pleasure of saluting Mrs. Cranceford. Some time has passed since I saw you, ma'am, and I hope you will pardon my absence."

The Major sprawled himself back with a laugh. Mrs. Cranceford, standing on the door sill, gave Gid a cool stare.

"Won't you please come in?" he asked, courteously waving his hand over the chair which he had just quitted.

"No, I thank you."

"Ah, I see you are surprised to see me in here. There was a time when it would have strained my boldness, but now it is a pleasure. I am here on business. To me business is a sweet morsel, and I delight myself with rolling it under my tongue. Ma'am, I have just signed a check. My dear old uncle, one of the most humane and charming of men, has been cruelly snatched from this life; and as he found it impossible to take his money with him, he left it to me."

"I hope you will make good use of it," she replied, with never a softening toward him.

"I am beginning well," he rejoined, surprised that she did not give him a kindlier look. "I am discharging my obligations, and before night I'll call on the rector and give him a check."

She smiled, but whether in doubt as to his sincerity or in commendation of his purpose he could not determine. But he took encouragement. "Yes, ma'am, and as I have now become a man of some importance, I am going to act accordingly. I am free to confess that my first endeavor shall be to gain your good opinion."

"And I'll freely give it, Mr. Batts, when I believe you merit it."

"To desire it, ma'am, is of itself a merit."

She laughed at this, and the Major laughed, too, for he saw that no longer should he be compelled to defend his fondness for the old fellow.

"I am more than willing to confess my mountain of faults," Gid went on, smiling, and his smile was not disagreeable. "I am more than willing to do this, and when I have—and which I now do—your Christian heart must forgive me."

She laughed and held out her hand, and with a gallantry that would have been reminiscent, even in old Virginia, he touched it with his lips.

"Come here, Margaret," said the Major, and when she turned toward him, smiling, he put his arms about her, pressed her to his breast and fondly kissed her.

CHAPTER XVIII

Mrs. Cranceford's surrender was not as complete as Gid's fancy had fore-pictured it; he had expected to see her bundle of prejudices thrown down like Christian's load; and therefore the dignity with which she looked upon the establishment of his honor was a disappointment to him, but she invited him to stay for dinner, and this argued that her reserve could not much longer maintain itself. With pleasure he recalled that she had given him her hand, but in this he feared that there was more of haughtiness than of generosity. And at the table, and later in the library, he was made to feel that after all she had accepted him merely on probation; still, her treatment of him was so different from what it had been, that he took the courage to build up a hope that he might at last subdue her. To what was passing the Major was humorously alive, and, too keenly tickled to sit still, he walked up and down the room, slyly shaking himself. Mrs. Cranceford asked Gid if he had read the book which she had loaned him, the "Prince of the House of David," and he answered that when at last he had fallen asleep the night before, the precious volume had dropped beside his pillow. There were some books which he read while sitting by the fire, and some whose stirring qualities moved him to walk about as he gulped their contents; but with a godly book he must lay himself down so that he might be more receptive of its soothing influence. Then he reviewed the book in question, and did it shrewdly. With the

Jewish maiden and the Roman centurion going to see the strange man perform the novel rite of baptism in the river of Jordan, he looked back upon the city of Jerusalem; and further along he pointed out Judas, plodding the dusty road—squat, sullen, and with a sneer at the marvel he was destined to see.

"I believe you have read it," the Major spoke up, still slyly shaking himself.

"Read it! Why, John, I have eaten it. I gad, sir—Pardon me, ma'am." With a nod she pronounced her forgiveness. The slip was but a pretense, foisted to change the talk to suit his purpose. "Ah," said he, "I have not yet weeded out all my idle words, and it grieves me when I am surprised by the recurrence of one which must be detestable; but, ma'am, I try hard, and there is always merit in a sincere trial."

"Yes, in a sincere trial," she agreed.

"Yes, ma'am; and—now there's John laughing at me fit to kill himself; and bless me, ma'am, you are laughing, too. Am I never to be taken seriously? Are you thus to titter true reformation out of countenance? But I like it. But we are never tired of a man so long as we can laugh at him; we may cry ourselves to sleep, but who laughs himself to slumber? Ma'am, are you going to leave us?" he asked, seeing that Mrs. Cranceford was on her feet. "But of course you have duties to look after, even though you might not be glad to escape an old man's gabble. I *call* it gabble, but I know it to be wisdom. But I beg pardon for seeming vanity."

A dignified smile was the only reply she made, but in the smile was legible the progress his efforts were making.

"John," he said, when she was gone, "that sort of a woman would have made a man of me."

"But perhaps that sort of a woman wouldn't have undertaken the job," the Major replied.

"Slow, John; but I guess you're right."

"I think so. Women may be persistent, but they are generally quick to recognize the impossible."

"Easy. But again I guess you're right. I gad, when the teachings of a man's mother leave him unfinished there isn't a great deal of encouragement for the wife. A man looks upon his wife as a part of himself, and a man will lie even to himself, John."

"By the way," the Major asked, sitting down, "have you seen that fellow Mayo since he came back?"

"Yes; I met him in the road once, but had no words with him."

"It would hardly do for me to have words with him," the Major replied; and after a moment of musing he added: "I understand that he's organizing the negroes, and that's the first step toward trouble. The negro has learned to withdraw his faith from the politician, but labor organization is a new thing to him, and he will believe in it until the bubble bursts. That fellow is a shrewd scoundrel and there's no telling what harm he may not project."

"Then why not hang him before he has time to launch his trouble? There's always a way to keep the cat from scratching you. Shoot the cat."

"No," said the Major, "that won't do. It would put us at a disadvantage."

"Yes; but I gad, our disadvantage wouldn't be as great as his. Nobody would be willing to swap places with a man that's hanged."

"That's all very well, but we would be the aggressors, and distant eyes would look upon him as a martyr."

"Yes, I know; but isn't it better to have one man looked on as a martyr than to have a whole community bathed in blood?"

"It might be better for us, but not for our children. A blood-bath may be forgotten, but martyrdom lives in the minds of succeeding generations."

"John, there spoke the man of business. You are always looking out for the future. I have agreed with myself to make the most of the present, and so far as the future is concerned, it will have to look out for itself—it always has. Was there ever a future that was not prepared to take care of itself? And is there a past that can be helped? Then let us fasten our minds to the present. Let me see. I wonder if we couldn't train a steer to gore that fellow to death. And I gad, that would do away with all possibility of martyrdom. What do you say?"

"Nothing more on that subject; but I can say something concerning another matter, and it will interest you more than the martyrdom of all history."

"Then out with it. I demand to be interested. But don't trifle with me, John. Remember that an old man's hide is thin."

"I'll not trifle with you; I'll startle you. Sixty years ago, the grandfather of Admiral Semmes made whisky in the Tennessee Mountains."

"But, John, that was a long time ago, and the old man is dead, and here we are alive. But he made whisky sixty years ago. What about it?"

"The brother of the admiral lives in Memphis," the Major continued, "and the other day he sent me a bottle of that whisky, run through a log before you were born."

Gid's mouth flew open and his eyes stuck out. "John," he said, and the restraint he put upon his voice rippled it, "John, don't tamper with the affections of an old and infirm man. Drive me off the bayou plantation, compel me to acknowledge and to feel that I am a hypercrite and a liar, but don't whet a sentiment and then cut my throat with it. Be merciful unto a sinner who worships the past."

He sat there looking upward, a figure of distress, fearing the arrival of despair. The Major laughed at him. "Don't knock me down with a stick of spice-wood, John."

The Major went to a sideboard, took therefrom a quaint bottle and two thin glasses, and placing them upon a round table, bowed to the bottle and said: "Dew of an ancient mountain, your servant, sir." And old Gid, with his mouth solemnly set, but with his eyes still bulging, arose, folded his arms, bowed with deep reverence, and thus paid his respects: "Sunshine, gathered from the slopes of long ago, your slave."

Mrs. Cranceford stepped in to look for something, and the play improvised by these two old boys was broken short off. The Major sat down, but Gid edged up nearer the table as if preparing to snatch the bottle. Upon the odd-shaped flask she cast a look of passing interest, and speaking to the Major she said:

"Oh, that's the whisky you got from Memphis. Don't drink it

all, please. I want to fill up the camphor bottle—"

Gid sat down with a jolt that jarred the windows, and she looked at him in alarm, fearing at the instant that death must have aimed a blow at him. "Camphor bottle!" he gasped. "Merciful heavens, ma'am,' fill up your camphor bottle with my heart's blood!"

At this distress the Major laughed, though more in sympathy than in mirth; and Mrs. Cranceford simply smiled as if with loathness she recognized that there was cause for merriment, but when she had quitted the room and gone to her own apartment, she sat down, and with the picture in her mind, laughed in mischievous delight.

"Help yourself," said the Major. Gid had spread his hands over the whisky as if to warm them in this liquidized soul of the past.

"Pour it out for me, John. And I will turn my back so as not to see how much you pour."

"Go ahead," the Major insisted.

"But I am shaken with that suggested profanation, that camphor bottle, and I'm afraid that I might spill a drop. But wait. I am also bold and will attempt it. Gods, look at that—a shredded sunbeam."

"Don't be afraid of it."

"I was waiting for you to say that, John. But it is reverence, and not fear. That I should have lived to see this day is a miracle. Shall I pour yours? There you are."

They stood facing each other. With one hand Gid held high

his glass, and with the other hand he pressed his heart. Their glasses clinked, and then they touched the liquor with their lips, sipped it, and Gid stretched his neck like a chicken. To have spoken, to have smacked his mouth, would have been profane. There is true reverence in nothing save silence, and in silence they stood. Gid was the first to speak, not that he had less reverence, but that he had more to say and felt, therefore, that he must begin earlier. "Like the old man of Israel, I am now ready to die," he said, as he put down his glass.

"Not until you have had another drink," suggested the Major.

"A further evidence, John, of your cool judgment. You are a remarkable man. Most anyone can support a sorrow, but you can restrain a joy, and in that is shown man's completest victory over self. No, I am not quite ready to die. But I believe that if a drop of this liquor, this saint-essence, had been poured into a camphor bottle, I should have dropped dead, that's all, and Peter himself would have complimented me upon the exquisite sensitiveness of my organization. Pour me just about two fingers—or three. That's it. If the commander of the Alabama had taken a few drinks of his grandfather's nectar, the Confederacy would have wanted a blockade runner."

"You don't mean to say that it would have softened his nerve, do you?"

"Oh, no; but his heart, attuned to sweet melody, would have turned from frowning guns to a beautiful nook in some river's bend, there to sing among flowers dripping with honey-dew. I gad, this would make an old man young before it could make him drunk."

The Major brought two pipes and an earthen jar of tobacco;

and with the smoke came musings and with the liquor came fanciful conceits. To them it was a pride that they could drink without drunkenness; in moderation was a continuous pleasure. When Gid arose to go, he took an oath that never had he passed so delightful a time. The Major pressed him to stay to supper. "Oh, no, John," he replied; "supper would spoil my spiritual flow. And besides, I am expecting visitors to-night."

He hummed a tune as he cantered down the road; and the Major in his library hummed the same tune as he stretched out his feet to the fire.

As Gid was passing the house of Wash Sanders, the endless invalid came out upon the porch and called him:

"Won't you 'light?"

"No, don't believe I've got time," Gid answered, slacking the pace of his horse. "How are you getting along?"

"Not at all. Got no relish for victuals. Don't eat enough to keep a chicken alive. Can't stand it much longer."

"Want to bet on it?" Gid cried.

"What's that?"

"I say I'm sorry to hear it."

"Glad to know that somebody sympathizes with me. Well, drop in some time and we'll take a chaw of tobacco and spit the fire out."

Nothing could have been more expressive of a welcome to Wash's house. To invite a man to sit until the fire was extinguished with the overflow of the quid was with him the topknot of courtesy.

"All right," Gid shouted back; and then to himself he said: "If I was sure that a drink of that old whisky would thrill him to death I'd steal it for him, but I'd have to be sure; I'd take no chances."

A horse came galloping up behind him. Dusk was falling and the old man did not at once recognize Mayo, the labor organizer of the negroes. But he knew the voice when the fellow spoke: "What's the weather about to do?"

"About to quit, I reckon," Gid answered.

"Quit what?"

"Quit whatever it's doing."

"Pretty smart as you go along, ain't you?"

"Yes, and when I stop, too."

"Strains you to answer a civil question, I see."

The old man turned in his saddle and jogged along facing the fellow, and some distance was covered before either of them spoke. "Are you trying to raise a row with me?" Gid asked. "I want to know for if you are I can save you a good deal of time and trouble."

"Sort of a time-saver," said Mayo.

"Yes, when I'm not a recruiter for eternity."

"I don't believe I follow you."

"Wish you would, or ride on ahead. Now look here," he added, "I just about know you when I see you, and as I don't make friends half as fast as I do enemies—in other words, as I am able to grasp a man's bad points quicker than I can catch his good ones—I would advise you not to experiment with me. You haven't come back here for the benefit of the community, and if we were not the most easy-going people in the world, we'd hang you and then speculate leisurely as to what might have been your aim in coming here."

Mayo grunted. He was a tall, big, stoop-shouldered fellow. He rode with his knees drawn up. He had a sort of "ducking" head, and his chin was long and pointed. He grunted and replied: "I guess this is a free country or at least it ought to be."

"Yes," Gid rejoined, still facing him, "but it won't be altogether free for such as you until the penitentiaries are abolished."

"Oh, I understand you, Mr. Batts. You are trying to work up a chance to kill me."

"Good guess; and you are trying to help me along."

"But I want to tell you that if you were to kill me you wouldn't live to tell the tale. I don't want any trouble with you. I'm not here to have trouble unless it's shoved on me. I am going to do one thing, however, trouble or no trouble; I am going to demand that the colored people shall have their rights."

"And at the same time I suppose you are going to demand that the white man shall not have his."

"No, won't demand that he shan't have his rights, but that he shan't have his way."

"Not have his way with his own affairs? Good. And now let me tell you something. Want to hear it?"

"I'm not aching to hear it."

"Well, I'll give it to you anyway. It's this: The first thing you know a committee of gentlemen will call on you and offer you the opportunity to make a few remarks, and after you have made them you will thereafter decline all invitations to speak. At the end of a rope the most talkative man finds a thousand years of silence. Long time for a man to hush, eh? Well, our roads split here."

"How do you know?"

"Because I turn to the right."

"But may be my business calls me over that way."

"Don't know about that, but I'm going to turn into this lane and I don't want you to come with me. Do you hear?"

Mayo did not answer. Gid turned into a road leading to the right, and looking back he saw that Mayo was riding straight ahead. "At any rate he ain't afraid to say what he thinks," the old man mused. "Got more nerve than I thought he had, and although it may make him more dangerous, yet it entitles him to more respect."

His horse's hoof struck into a patch of leaves, heaped beneath a cottonwood, and from the rustling his ears, warmed by the old liquor, caught the first bars of a tune he had known in his youth; and lifting high his voice he sang it over and over again. He passed a negro cabin whence often had proceeded at night the penetrating cry of a fiddle, and it was night now but no fiddle sent forth its whine. A dog shoved open the door, and by the fire light within the old man saw a negro sitting with a gun across his lap, and beside him stood two boys, looking with rapture upon their father's weapon. Throughout the neighborhood had spread a report that the negroes were meeting at night to drill, and this glance through a door gave life to what had been a shadow.

He rode on, and his horse's hoof struck into another patch of leaves, but no tune arose from the rustle. The old man was thinking. In a field of furrowed clouds the moon was struggling, and down the sandy road fell light and darkness in alternating patches. Far away he saw a figure stepping from light into darkness and back again into light. Into the deep shadow of a vine-entangled tree he turned his horse, and here he waited until he heard footsteps crunching in the sand, until he saw a man in the light that lay for a moment in the road, and then he cried:

"Hello, there, Jim Taylor!"

"Is that you, Uncle Gideon?"

"Yes, Gideon's band of one. Come over here a moment."

"I will as soon as I can find you. What are you doing hiding out in the dark? The grand jury ain't in session."

"No, I gad, but something else is," he replied.

Jim came forward and put his hand on the horn of the old man's saddle, which as an expert he did in spite of the shying of the horse; and then he asked: "Well, what is it, Uncle Gideon?"

"You've heard the rumor that the negroes are drilling at night."

"Yes, what of it?"

"It's a fact, that's what there is of it. Just now I rode quite a ways with Mayo and he was inclined to be pretty sassy; and right back there I looked into Gabe Little's cabin and saw him with a gun across his lap."

"Well, what of that? Haven't the negroes had guns ever since the war, and hasn't a man got the right to sit with his gun across his lap? Uncle Gideon, I'm afraid you've been putting too much new wine into an old bottle."

"Soft, Jimmie; it was old liquor, sixty years at least. But I gad, it strikes me that you are pretty glib to-night. You must have heard something."

"No, not since Mrs. Cranceford got the letter, but that was enough to last me a good while."

"Didn't hear about my bereavement, did you?"

"What, you bereaved, Uncle Gideon? How did it happen?"

"At the imperious beck and call of nature, Jimmie. My uncle died and inflicted on me money enough to make a pretense of paying my debts, and I've made such a stagger that even Mrs. Cranceford has admitted me into the out-lying districts of her good opinion. But that's got nothing to do with the business in hand. Let's go back yonder and find out why that negro sits there suckling his gun to sleep."

"But if he suckles it to sleep there's no harm in it, Uncle Gideon."

"Ah, clod-head, but it may have bad dreams and wake up with a cry. Let's go back there."

"Are you in earnest?"

"As earnest as a last will and testament."

"Then let me tell you that I'll do nothing of the sort. You don't catch me prowling about a man's house at night, and you wouldn't think of such a thing if you were strictly sober."

"Jimmie, you never saw me drunk."

"No, but I've seen you soberer that you are now."

"An unworthy insinuation, Jimmie. But having great respect for your plodding judgment, I will not go to the negro's cabin, but will proceed rather to my own shanty. And I want you to come with me. Tom Cranceford and Sallie Pruitt will be there and in the shine of the fire we'll cut many a scollop. What do you say?"

"Uncle Gideon, don't you know how strongly opposed Mrs. Cranceford is to Tom's—"

"Bah, law-abiding calf. They are going to marry anyway, so what's the difference? Jimmie, the most useless man in the world is the fellow that keeps just within the law. But perhaps it isn't your law-abiding spirit so much as it is your fear. In blind and stupid obedience there is a certain sort of gallantry, and in trotting to Mrs. Cranceford's cluck you may be wise."

"It's not that I'm afraid of offending her," the giant said. "The girl is too good for Tom any day, or for any of us when it comes to that, but the distress of his mother haunts me, and I don't want that girl's affection for Tom to haunt me too. I don't want to see them together if I can help it. One haunt at a time is enough. But I tell you this, if it should come to a question I would decide in favor of the girl."

"Jimmie, you are improving. Yes, I am doing you great good. I found your mind an insipid dish and I have sprinkled it with salt and pepper. You are right. Always decide in favor of the young, for the old have already had their disappointments. Well, I'll go. Lift your paw. My horse can't move out from under its weight."

"All right," said the giant, laughing and stepping back. "By the way," he added, "tell Tom to be sure and meet me at the landing at two o'clock to-morrow. We are going down to New Orleans."

"What, alone? I ought to go along to take care of you. I could steer you away from all the bad places and by this means you would naturally stumble on the good ones. I'll see you when you get back."

At home the old man had lighted his fire and was listening to its cheerful crackle when his visitors came, laughing. With a boisterous shout Tom kicked the door open, and when the girl remonstrated with him, he grabbed her and kissed her.

"That's all right," old Gid cried. "One of these days the penitentiary doors will open for you without being kicked in. Ah, delightful to see you, my dear," he said, bowing to the girl; "refreshing to see you, although you come with a scamp. Sit down over there. I gad, you are a bit of sunshine that has lost its way in the night."

About her head she had wound a scarf of red yarn, and as she stood taking it off, with the fire-light dancing among the kinks of her flax-like hair, the old man stepped forward to help her.

"Hands off," said Tom. "Don't touch her."

"Wolfish protector of a lamb," the old man replied, "I ought to throw you out; but it is not my mission to cast out devils."

The girl sat down on a bench and Tom took a seat beside her; and with many a giggle and a "quit that, now," they picked at each other. Old Gid, in his splint-bottomed chair, leaned back against the wall and feasted his eyes upon their antics. "Kittens," said he, "I will get you a string and a button. Ah, Lord, I was once a delicious idiot."

"And you've simply lost your deliciousness," Tom replied.

"Ah, and in its place took up age. But with it came wisdom, Thomas."

"But didn't it come too late?"

"The wise utterance of a foolish youth," said the old man. "Yes, Thomas, it came too late. Wisdom is not of much use to an old codger. He can't profit by it himself and nobody wants his advice. Did I ever tell you about the girl I loved? Ah, she was glorious. June was in her mouth and October fell out of her hair."

"And you didn't marry her because she was poor, eh?"

"No, but because she was rich, Jimmie. She wanted me not; and she married a wealthy fool and the imbecile made her happy. I could almost forgive her for not loving me, for I was a mate on a steamboat, but to let that fool make her happy—it was too much and I cast her out of my mind. But when is your wedding to take place? In the sweet light of a distant moon or within the sunshine of a few days?"

"Hanged if I know."

"Tom!" cried the girl, putting her hands over his mouth, "that's no way to talk."

"I said it to make you do that," he replied, his voice latticed by her fingers and sounding afar off. He took her hands and pressed them to his cheek.

"A pretty picture, and I'll long remember you as you now sit on that bench," said the old man. "Sallie, how old are you?" he asked.

"I don't know, sir. Pap and mother couldn't put it down 'cause they didn't know how to figger, and when I got so I could figger a little they had dun forgot the year and the day of the month. Most of the time when I'm by myself I feel old enough, but sometimes Uncle Wash calls me foolish and then I'm awful young. But Aunt Martha never calls me foolish 'cause I help her in the kitchen."

There came a scratching at the threshold. The old man got out of his tilted chair and opened the door, and a dog, prancing in, lay down in front of the fire, with his nose between his outstretched paws.

"What a pretty dog," said the girl, and with a look out of one eye and with a slight wag of the tail the dog acknowledged the compliment.

"Oh, he's gallant," Gid replied, sitting down. "And he knows when a truth has been told about him."

"No good at hunting, is he?" Tom asked.

"He is not a sportsman," Gid answered. "He pays his keep with companionship. I sit here and read him to sleep nearly every night. He tries to keep awake, but he can't. But as long as I read a lively book he'll lie there and look up at me as if he enjoys it, and I believe he does, but 'Benton's Thirty Years in the American Senate' will knock him most any time. And old Whateley's logic makes him mighty drowsy. I reckon you cubs have been to supper. If you haven't you may make yourselves at home and cook something. Old Aunt Liza cooks for me, out there in the other room, but she's generally away in the service of her church and then I have to shift for myself."

"We've been to supper," the girl spoke up, "but if you want something to eat I'll cook it."

"Bless your life, not a bite," the old man protested. "To eat now would canker a memory. I took sacrament over at the Major's. Now, I'm going to lean back here and I may talk or I may drop off to sleep, and in either event just let me go. But if I doze off don't wake me, not even when you get ready to leave. Just pull the door to and that's all."

"Ain't you afraid to sleep here all by yourself?" the girl asked. "I'd be afraid somebody'd slip in and grab me."

"I could scarcely blame any one for grabbing you, my dear," the old man replied, smiling upon her, "but as for myself, the grabber would get the worst of it."

A long time they sat and talked of neighborhood happenings, the death of a burly man who it was never supposed could die before Wash Sanders was laid away; they talked of the growing dissatisfaction among the negroes, of the church built by Father Brennon, of the trip to be taken to New Orleans by Jim and Tom. The fire-light died down. A chunk fell and the dog jumped up with a sniff and a sneeze. Old Gideon took no notice, for leaning back against the wall he was softly snoring.

"Let us leave him just as he is," said Tom.

"But it looks cruel," the girl replied.

"He suffers from sleeplessness; to wake him would be more cruel. Let's do as he told us."

The girl put the bench out of the way, that he might not fall over it in the dark; and out of the room they tip-toed and silently they closed the door. By the hand he led her to the road, and with a coo and a song they strolled homeward. The clouds were scattered and acres of light lay on the cleared land; but the woods were dark and the shadows were black, and he walked with his arm about her. They heard the galloping of a horse and stepped aside to let the rider pass, and when he had passed, with his head in the moonlight and his horse in the dark, the young man said: "I know that fellow."

"Why didn't you speak to him?" she asked.

"Because it wouldn't do for me to have any words with him. He's the man that's trying to organize the negroes."

He left her at Wash Sanders' gate; he heard her feet upon the steps, and looking back he caught the kiss she threw at him.

CHAPTER XIX

A steamboat ride to New Orleans will never lose its novelty. Romance lies along the lower river. The land falls away and we look down upon fields bounded by distant mist, and beyond that dim line one's fancy gallops riotously. Not alone the passenger, but the seasoned captain of the boat stands musing and motionless, gazing upon the scene. In his mind he could carry the form and the rugged grandeur of a mountain; upon a crag he could hang his recollection, but this flat endlessness is ever an unencompassed mystery.

The wind from the gulf was soft, and the two friends stood on the hurricane-deck, charmed with a familiar view.

"It is just as new to me now as it was when I was a boy, coming along here with my father," said the giant. "And yet I don't see what makes it interesting, no woods, nothing but a house here and there."

"It always makes me think I'm going over the flat side of the globe, and I catch myself wondering what's just beyond," Tom replied. "There's the city 'way round yonder. How long do you want to stay?"

"I don't know exactly."

"Got any particular business down here?"

"No," he said, hesitatingly. "None that I know of."

"Just pleasure, is it?"

"Well, I reckon we might call it that."

"Might call it that? But I know why I'm here. I've come because you wanted me to. There is nothing going on that I care to see. What is it you're after?"

"Oh, just want to look around a little."

"All right, old fellow, I'm with you, but as soon as you get tired of looking around I wish you'd let me know. It seems to me that I've been gone a month already. You know why."

"Yes, I know; but you've got a consolation that I never had—you know what to expect when you get back."

"Yes, that's true, and may be you'll know what to expect one of these days."

From the museful distance the giant removed his gaze and upon the boy at his side he bent a kindly look. "I have been reading a good deal of late," he said, "and old Gid has told me that I am improving, but I have found no book to speak a word of comfort to me. I took the heartache away back yonder—but we won't talk about it. We'll poke around down here a day or two and then go home."

"But hang it, I thought you came to enjoy yourself and not to conjure up things to make you sad."

"You are right, and you shan't hear any more sad talk out

of me."

It was early in the forenoon when they stepped ashore and stood upon the old levee. The splendid life of the Mississippi steamboat is fading, but here the glow lingers, the twilight at the close of a fervid day. No longer are seen the gilded names of famous competitors, "The Lee," "The Natchez," but unheralded boats are numerous, and the deck-hands' chorus comes with a swell over the water, and the wharf is a jungle of trade.

In the French market they drank black coffee, listening to the strange chatter about them, and then aimlessly they strolled away.

"What's your programme?" the boy asked.

"Haven't any."

"Do you want to call on any of the cotton buyers?"

"No, don't care to see them."

"All right; I'll walk until you say quit."

And thus they passed the day, with strolling about, halting to look at an old tiled roof, a broken iron gate, a wrought iron balcony, a snail-covered garden wall; and when evening was come they went to a hotel to rest; but no sooner had night fallen than they went out again to resume their walk.

"Look here," said Tom, beginning to lag, "I don't want to kick, but I'd just like to know why I am fool enough to walk all day like a mule on a tread-mill?"

"You said you'd walk with me."

"Said I would! Haven't I?"

"Yes," the giant drawled, "in a manner."

"If I haven't walked I don't know what you call walking. You have made a machine of me, a corn-planter. Would you mind telling me where we are going now?"

"I confess I don't know," the giant answered.

"Then let us look around and find out. Right now I'd rather be in old Gid's house, sitting with somebody on a bench—and I'm going back to-morrow. What fun is there in poking about this way like a couple of gawks? You even pull me away from the supper table to tramp up and down these streets. Hang it, I don't want to see people. Every face I see is—"

"A disappointment," said the giant.

"Then why do you take the crowded side of the street? Let's go in here and sit down a moment."

They had halted in front of a music hall. From within proceeded the husky song of a worn-out negro minstrel.

"You may go in but I'll walk on," Jim replied. "It's nothing but a dive. I'll go on down to the corner and wait for you. Don't stay long."

Jim strode away and Tom went into the beer hall. At the far end was a stage, and on it stood the minstrel, dimmed by intervening tobacco smoke. The floor was covered with damp saw-dust. The place was thronged with a motley crowd, sailors, gamblers, with here and there a sprinkle of wayward respectability. Painted girls attended the tables and everywhere was the slopping of beer and the stench of the cigarette.

Tom was about to turn away when the sight of a company gathered about a table halted him; and through the smoke his vision leaped and rested upon—Louise. There was a rush, an over-turning of a table, the toppling over of a tipsy man, and Tom stood confronting her. In a loud voice he cried: "What the devil are you doing here?"

She got up and held out her hand, but resentment entered her mind and she drew it back. "What are *you* doing here?" she replied. "I've as much right here as you have."

"I'll show you about that!" he roared, his anger lifting his voice high above the grumble and the sharp clack of the place. "I'll drag you out!"

Beside her sat a solemnly-respectable man, and up he got and quietly said: "Your language is most insulting, sir."

Tom did not wait to weigh the remark; indeed he did not hear it, for like a bull-dog in a fury he lunged at the quiet man's throat, laid hold of his collar, shoved him off to arm's length, and struck him, but the blow glanced and the man jerked away. And then amid loud cries, the over-turning of tables and the smashing of glasses, the furious youngster felt himself seized by many hands. But he was a tiger and they could not bear him to the floor. He broke loose and sprawled one man upon the saw-dust. Others rushed upon him and again he was in a tangle and a tug, but he tore himself from their hands, got a square blow at the proprietor of the house and knocked him senseless. For a moment he was free, and this moment was not left unimproved. From an upturned table he wrenched a leg, and swinging it above his head he cleared his way to a side door, and snatching it open, he sprung out into a small court, just as the police were entering at the front of the house. In the court a dim light was burning; at the end, but a few yards away, was a rusty iron gate, and whether or not it was locked he never knew, for throwing down his weapon he laid hold of a bar and with a jerk he tore the gate from its rust-eaten hinges, threw it against a wall and was out in the street. Now he ran, through an open space, into another street, and then he walked, panting, looking back. It must have been difficult to explain the cause of the disturbance for the police had not followed him. He halted under a lamp hung above a narrow doorway. His hat was gone, his coat was torn, and the bosom of his shirt was in shreds. The short street was deserted, but he fancied that he heard footsteps, and quickly he walked to a corner, and turning, saw Jim standing under a lamp-post not far away. The giant was not looking toward him, and not hearing his easy approach, did not turn his head until Tom was almost within the shade-rim of the lamp.

"Why, what the deuce have you been doing?" the giant cried, reaching him at a stride. "You look like a drowned rat, and your neck is clawed. What have you been doing?"

"Row," the boy panted.

"In that place? Come back and we'll clean it out. Come on."

"No," said Tom, "let's get away from here. I've got something to tell you. Let's circle round here somewhere and get a hat. I'll tell you when we get back to the hotel, and you won't care to walk any more to-night after I've told you."

Jim might have been burning to know more, but he said nothing, for dogged patience was a part of his heroism. He took the boy's arm and led him away, to a place where a hat was bought, and thence to the hotel; and not until they were shut in a room did Tom attempt to tell his story. And it was even then some minutes before he could proceed. His anger was gone and sorrow was upon him. Several times he choked. And then he told his story. With hard steps the giant walked about the room, saying not a word; but he drooped as he halted at the window, as he stood looking out upon the glimmering lights, far below.

"You said I wouldn't want to walk to-night, but I must," he spoke, and his voice had a smothered sound. "I am going out to look for her. And now you know why I have been walking all day, gazing at the faces in the crowd." He had turned from the glimmering lights and was looking at Tom. "I traced that letter she wrote, and in my mind I settled that it must have come from this place. But I didn't tell your mother what I suspected; I kept it to myself."

"If you go out again I'll go with you, Jim."

"No, I insist upon going alone."

He went out; and when he returned, just before the dawn, he found the boy asleep on a chair. He took him up, put him upon a bed and sat himself down at a window; and when Tom awoke, along toward ten o'clock, the giant was still sitting there.

"Jim."

"Well."

"How long have you been in?"

"Don't know."

"You didn't—didn't find her?"

"No. I went to the place where you had the fight—wish to the Lord I had been with you—but of course couldn't learn anything. I was—was afraid to ask about her. But I tramped around all night, and I went into all sorts of places, looking for her, and all the time afraid that I might find her. God, what am I talking about! Afraid of finding her! Why, she couldn't be in a place where—where she oughtn't to be."

"But she was!" the boy cried, bounding out upon the floor. "She was and—Great God, I can hardly believe it, I don't realize it! I have been so swallowed up that I haven't thought about her much lately—she's crazy, Jim. Oh, she must be. She was the purest-minded girl—"

The giant stopped him with an uplifting of his ponderous hand. "Don't say any more. Don't say she *was* pure-minded. She *is* pure-minded. I will find her and she shall tell me—"

"She can't tell you anything to clear herself, Jim. She's lost—she's crazy."

"She's an angel," said the giant.

"My dear Jim, she's my sister and I loved her, but angels can't go—"

"Don't say it."

"I won't, but don't you be foolish. Truth is truth, and we have to look at it whether we want to or not." He walked up and down the room. "Who would have thought that such a thing could happen?" he went on. "It's a dream. But why did she leave home when she knew how much we all loved her? What made her run away from you when she knew how you loved her? Jim, I'm going home to-day. Are you coming with me?"

"No, I'm going to stay here and look for her."

"And when you have found her she'll treat you as she did me. She'll say she has as much right there as you have. I don't believe it's any use. Better come home with me."

"No, I'm going to look for her, and if she'll marry me I'll bring her home."

"Jim, she is my sister, but—I won't say it. I love her, but I would rather have seen her dead than where I saw her last night. I'm going home."

"Wait a moment." For a time he pondered and then he said: "You may tell your mother, but don't tell the Major."

"But why should it be kept from him? He ought to know it. We'll have to tell him some time."

"Some time, may be, but not now, and don't you even hint it to him, and don't you tell Sallie. Don't tell any one but your mother. Do you hear?"

"Yes, and I reckon you're right. I'll do as you tell me. Well, it's time and I'm going."

Jim went with him to the levee, saw him on a boat and then resumed his search throughout the town. But he asked no questions; and three days later when he went aboard the home-bound boat, he knew no more than he had known the night when the boy had told his story.

CHAPTER XX

The night was rainy and a fierce wind was blowing. The Major and his wife were by the fire in the sitting-room, when there came a heavy tread upon the porch, but the knock that fell upon the door was gentle. They knew who had come, and the door was opened for Jim Taylor. Quietly he responded to their greeting, and with both hands he took off his slouch hat, went to the fireplace and over the blaze shook it.

"Put myself in mind of a wet dog," he said. "Didn't think to shake outside. How are you all getting along?"

He was looking at Mrs. Cranceford, but the Major answered him. "In the same old way. Tilt that cat out of the rocking-chair and sit down."

"Have you heard of the death of Mrs. Wash Sanders?" Mrs. Cranceford asked, fearing that the Major might get ahead of her with this piece of news, but all along determined that he should not.

"No, I haven't," he said; but his want of surprise was not satisfying, and Mrs. Cranceford said: "I mean Mrs. Wash Sanders."

"Yes, I know; but this is the first I've heard of it. I came from the boat right up here. So the poor woman's dead? She never knew anything but hard work. How long was she sick? Shouldn't think she could take the time to be sick long, poor soul."

"She was not in bed more than two days. It was awful, the way she suffered. And all the time Wash was whining that he couldn't eat anything, as if anybody cared. I never was so provoked at a man in my life. I'd like to know who cares whether he eats another bite or not. Actually, I believe he thought the neighbors had come to sympathize with him instead of to nurse his wife. And when she was dead he went about blubbering that he couldn't live but a few days."

"He'll outlive us all," said the Major. "He told us yesterday that he was threatened with convulsions, and Gid swore that a convulsion was about the last thing he ought to fear, that he was too lazy to entertain such an exertion."

In this talk Jim felt not even the slightest interest. He wanted to talk about Louise. But not in Mrs. Cranceford's manner nor in her eyes when she looked straight at him was there a hint that Tom had told her that the girl had been seen. Perhaps the boy had decided to elect him to this unenviable office. The Major asked him about his trip, but he answered as if he cared not what he said; but when shortly afterward the Major went out, Taylor's unconcern fell from him and he stood up and in tremulous anxiousness looked at Mrs. Cranceford, expecting her to say something. Surely Tom had told her nothing, for she quietly smiled at him as he stood there, awkwardly and distressfully fumbling with himself.

"I have a letter from her," she said.

Taylor sat down hard. "A letter from her!"

"Yes; received it this morning."

"But has Tom told you anything?"

"Yes; everything."

"And she has written to you since then?"

"Yes; I will show you." On a corner of the mantel-piece was a work-box, and unlocking it, she took out a letter and handed it to him. "Read it," she said, "and if you hear the Major coming, put it away. Some references in it would have to be explained, and so I have decided not to let him see it."

He took the letter, and standing where the light from the hanging lamp fell brightest, read the following:

"My Dear Mother:—By this time Tom must have told you of our meeting. And what a meeting it was. He was worse than an orang-outang, but I must say that I admire his courage, and I struggled to help him when he was in the thick of his fight, but my friends tore me away, realizing that flight was our only redemption. Of course you will wonder why I was in such a place, and I don't know that I can explain in a satisfactory manner to you, and surely not to father. I would have introduced Tom to my friends had he given me time, but it appears that he was in too much of a hurry to attend upon the demands of politeness. Fight was boiling in his blood and it had to bubble out. Mother, I was with a slumming party. Do you know what a slumming party is? It is a number of respectable people whom curiosity leads into the resorts of crime and vice. Society thinks that it makes one wiser, and that to know the aspect of depravity does not make one less innocent. But I know that you will not approve of a slumming party, and I cannot say that I do. The Rev. H. Markham, whose sermons you must have read, was with me. As the champion of virtue he has planned and executed an invasion of the haunts of iniquity, and his weekly discourses here are very popular, particularly with women. Well, he was sitting beside me, and I have since thought that it must have been a great shock to his dignity when Tom struck him; but his greatest solicitude was the fear that the occurrence might be spread by the newspapers, and to keep it out was his first care. That night on business I left the city, and I write this in a quiet, Arcadian neighborhood. It is with pleasure that I feel myself a success in the work which I have chosen. What work? you naturally ask. But that is my secret, and I must hold it just a little longer."

Here several lines were erased and a fresh start taken. "I have longed to look upon the dear faces at home; but mingled with my love is a pride. I am determined to make something of myself. Simply to be an honest, patient, upright woman, in love with her home, is no longer enough. Life demands more than this, or at least woman demands it of life. And to be somebody calls for sacrifice as well as ability and determination. Absence from home is my sacrifice, and what my effort is you shall know in due time. It will surprise you, and in this to me will lie a delight. My associates tell me that I am different from anyone else, but this difference they put down as an individuality, and success in my field is won only by the individual. Within two weeks from this day I shall be with you, and then my little ant-hill of mystery will be torn to pieces. I am going to show you all how I love you; I am going to prove to you that what has appeared odd and unlady-like were but leadings to my development."

More lines were erased, and then the letter thus proceeded:

"For some time I have had it in mind to make Sallie Pruitt a present, but as I have no idea as to what she might like best, I enclose twenty dollars, which you will please give to her. Do you see my hero often? I think of him, dream of him, and my heart will never know a perfect home until his love has built a mansion for it."

The letter was fluttering in the giant's hand. "Who—who—what does she mean?"

"She means you, stupid!" Mrs. Cranceford cried.

He looked up, dazed; he put out his hand, he grabbed his hat, he snatched the door open and was out in the wind and the rain.

CHAPTER XXI

With rain-soaked sand the road was heavy, and to walk was to struggle, but not so to the giant treading his way homeward. Coming, he had felt the opposition of the wind, the rain and the mushy sand, but returning he found neither in the wind nor in the sand a foe to progress. His heart was leaping, and with it his feet were keeping pace. In his hand he held the letter; and feeling it begin to cool in his grasp, he realized that the rain was beating upon it; so, holding in common with all patient men the instincts of a woman, he put the wet paper in his bosom and tightly buttoned his coat about it. Suddenly he halted; the pitiful howling of a dog smote his ear. At the edge of a small field lying close to the road was a negro's cabin, and from that quarter came the dog's distressful outcry. Jim stepped up to the fence and listened for any human-made noise that might proceed from the cabin, but there came none—the place was dark and deserted. "They have gone away and left him shut up somewhere," he mused, as he began to climb the fence. The top rail broke under his weight, and his mind flew back to the day when he had seen Louise in the road, confronted by the burly leader of a sheepfold, for then with climbing a fence he had broken the top rail.

He found the dog shut in a corn-crib, and the door was locked. But with a jerk he pulled out the staple, thinking not upon the infraction of breaking a lock, but glad to be of service even to a hound.

"Come out, old fellow," he called, and he heard the dog's tail thrashing the corn husks. "Come on."

The dog came to the door, licking at the hand of his rescuer; and Jim was about to help him to the ground when a lantern flashed from a corner of the crib. "What are you doing here?" a voice demanded.

A white man stepped forward and close behind him a negro followed. "What are you doing here?" the white man again demanded.

"Getting a dog out of trouble."

"Getting yourself into trouble, you'd better say. What right have you to poke about at night, breaking people's locks?"

"None at all, I am forced to acknowledge. I hardly thought of what I was doing. My only aim was to help the dog."

"That will do to tell."

"Yes, I think so. And by the way, what right have you to ask so many questions? You don't live here."

"But he does," the white man replied, swinging his lantern toward the negro. "Gabe Little lives here."

"That you, Gabe?" Taylor asked.

"Yas, whut de white folks has left o' me."

"All right. You are well enough acquainted with me to know

that I wouldn't break a lock—"

"But you have, sir," the white man insisted.

"Not exactly; but I have drawn the staple. By the way, whose dog is this?" The dog had jumped out and was frisking about Taylor's legs. "It's a setter and doesn't belong to you, Gabe."

"Dat's fur me ter say, sah," the negro sullenly replied.

"That so? Well, I guess I'll keep him until I find out his owner."

"That's neither here nor there!" the white man almost shouted. "The question is, what right have you got to go to a man's house at night and break his lock?"

"None, I tell you; and I'm not only willing to pay all damages, but will answer to the law."

"The law!" and this time he shouted. "Law to protect a negro's lock? Let us hear no more about the law. What we want is justice, and we're going to have it, sooner or later."

"Who are you, anyway?" the giant asked. "Oh, yes, you are Mr. Mayo, I believe. Well, I'll bid you good-night."

"Wait. You have invaded this man's premises and committed a violence."

"That's a fact, and I'm sorry for it."

"Yes, you are now, but how will you feel about it to-morrow? You'll forget all about it, and that's the way the colored man is treated in this infernal state. No, Gabe," he quickly added, taking hold of the negro's arm, "Put it up. The time ain't ripe."

The negro had drawn a knife, opening it with a spring, and with a loud snap he closed it. "We mustn't be the first to strike, although they break into our houses," Mayo said; and then speaking to Taylor he added: "You may go."

The giant threw back his head and laughed. "I may go. Why, if it wasn't for the fact that I'm feeling particularly happy to-night, I'd mash your mouth for that. I should think that your poor fool there would teach you better than to talk to me that way. But I'll be a better friend to you than you have taught him to be—I'll give you some very useful advice. If you should ever see me coming along the road, turn back or climb the fence, for I might not be in as good humor as I'm in now."

He whistled and strode away, with the dog trotting at his heels; and by the time he gained the road the occurrence had almost wholly passed out of his mind, so fondly did his heart leap at the thought of the letter in his bosom.

Upon reaching a gate that opened into his meadow, he looked about and whistled for the dog, but the setter was gone. "You were howling for your master," the giant said, "and the greatest service I could do you was to let you go to him. All right, old fellow, we are both happier for having met."

He went into the house, lighted his lamp, sat down, read the letter; he went out and stood under the weeping-willow. "If I am foolish," he said, "it is delicious to be a fool, and God pity the wise. But I don't know what to do with myself. Yes, I do; I'll go over and see old Gideon."

He considered not the increasing rain, the dreariness of the road, the moanful wind in the tops of the trees; he felt that to be alone was to suppress a part of his happiness, that his light and talkative heart must seek a hearing for the babbling of its joy. So off he strode, and as he climbed over a fence, he laughingly jolted himself upon the top rail to see whether it would break. It did not, and he laughed to find a stick of old timber strong enough to support his weight. He called himself a lumbering fool and laughed again, sitting there with the rain beating upon him.

A short distance down the road was a wagon-maker's shop, and against the outside wall a ladder was leaned. He thought of the ladder as he bore to the edge of the road to avoid the deep ruts cut by the cotton-wagons, and fearful that he might pass under it and thus invite ill luck, he crossed to the other side. He smiled at this weakness, instilled by the negroes, but he did not recross the road until he had passed far beyond the shop. The old black mammy was lovable and affectionate, but she intimidated man with many a superstition.

CHAPTER XXII

In old Gid's house a light was burning, and as the giant drew near, he caught a fragment of a flat-boatman's song. He made no noise, but a dog inside scented his approach and announced it with a whimsical bark. Gid opened the door.

"Why, here's Jim Taylor, as wet as a drowned bear. Come in."

Sitting by the fire was the Major, with his coat off and his shirt collar unbuttoned.

"Why, James," said he, "you are making the rounds to-night. Sit down here and dry yourself. And look at you, mud up to your knees. Why do you tramp about this way? Why don't you ride?"

"Too heavy," the giant answered.

"Then, I gad," Gid replied, dragging his bench from against the wall and sitting down upon it, "I know I'd ride. Do men ride for their own comfort or for the horse's? And what difference do a few extra pounds make to a horse? Why, if you were a horse somebody would ride you. You are not fat, Jim; you are just big. And a horse doesn't mind a well-proportioned fellow; it's the wabbling fat man that riles him.

I owned a horse once that would have been willing to go without corn a whole week for a chance to kick a fat man; and I put it down as an unreasonable cruelty until I found out that he had once belonged to a fellow that weighed three hundred pounds."

"And you afterward owned him," said the Major, winking at Jim.

"That's what I said, John."

"Now, Gid, I don't want to appear captious, but are you sure you ever owned a horse?"

"I bought that horse, John. I confess that it was with borrowed money, but under the law he was mine. Ah, Lord," he sighed, "self-imposed frankness will be gone when I am taken from you. And yet I get no credit."

"No credit!" cried the Major. "Credit has kept you from starving."

"Tip-toe, John; my nerves are tight-strung. Would have starved! A befitting reproach thrown at genius. Look up there!" he shouted, waving his hand at the shelf whereon were piled his dingy books. "They never owned a horse and they lived on credit, but they kept the world from starving to death. And this reminds me that those sweet potatoes must be about done. Your name is among the coals, Jim; we've got enough for all hands. Wish we had some milk, but I couldn't get any. Dogs couldn't catch the cow. You hear of cows giving milk. Mine don't—I gad, I have to grab her and take it away from her; and whenever you see milk in my house you may know it's the record of a fight and that the cow got the worst of it."

Jim sat striving to think of something to say. The presence of the Major had imposed a change in his forecast. His meeting of Mayo and the negro suddenly recurred to him, and quietly he related the adventure. But the Major and Gid were not quiet with hearing it.

"You ought to have cut his throat!" Gid exclaimed. "To-morrow get your gun and shoot him down—both of them, like dogs. Who ever heard of such a thing, saying to a gentleman, 'now you may go!' I gad, I'll go with you, and we'll shoot 'em down."

"No," said the Major, and now with his hands behind him he was slowly pacing the floor. "That won't do."

"Why won't it do?" Gid cried. "Has the time come when a white man must stand all sorts of abuse simply because he is white? Must he stand flat-footed and swallow every insult that a scoundrel is pleased to stuff into his mouth?"

The Major sat down. "Let me remind you of something," he said. "For the average man, under ordinary circumstances, it is enough to have simple justice on his side, but on our side we must have more than justice. No people in the world were ever situated as we now are, for even by our brothers we shall be deemed wrong, no matter which way we turn."

"Ah," Gid cried, "then what's the use of calculating our turn? If we are to be condemned anyway, what's the—"

"Hold on a moment," the Major struck in, "and I will tell you. Sentiment is against us; literature, with its roots running back into the harsh soil of politics, is against us; and—"

"No measured oratory, John. Get down on the ground."

"Wait, I tell you!" the Major demanded. "I must get to it in my own way. If your advice were followed, we should never be able to elect another president. The bloody shirt would wave from every window in the North, and from the northern point of view, justly so; and reviewed even by the disinterested onlooker, we have not been wholly in the right."

"The deuce we haven't!" Gid shouted, his eyes bulging.

"No, not wholly; we couldn't be," the Major continued. "As self-respecting men, as Anglo-Saxons, we could not submit to the domination of former slaves. It was asking too much. We had ruled the nation, and though we were finally overpowered, we could not accept the negro as a ruler."

"John, I know all that as well as you do; we have talked it many a time, but what I want to get at is this: Has a man the right to resent an insult? I was never cruel to a negro. I like him in his place, like him better than I do the average white man, to tell the plain truth, for between him and me there is the tie of irresponsibility, of shiftlessness; but I don't want him to insult me; don't want to stand any more from him than I would from a white man. You spoke of not being able to elect another president. Why should we put up with so much merely to say that a democrat is president? It doesn't make much difference who's president, foreign nations keep on insulting us just the same. I'd like to see a chief magistrate with nerve enough to say to the South, 'Boys, go over and grab off Mexico.' That's me."

The Major laughed. "That's me, too," he replied.

"We ought to sweeten this country with Cuba," said Jim, with his mind on the letter in his bosom.

"Yes," Gid replied, raising his hand, "that's what we ought to do, and—" His hand fell, and he wheeled about and seized a poker. "I'll bet a thousand dollars the potatoes are burned up," he said. "Just look there," he added, raking out the charred remains of what was to be a feast. "That's the way it goes. The devil titters when men argue. Well, it can't be helped," he went on. "I did my part. If we had settled upon killing that fellow Mayo, everything would have been all right. He has not only insulted us but has robbed us as well."

"To tell you the truth," said the Major, "I'm glad I'm relieved of the trouble of eating."

"John, don't say that, for when a Southern man loses his appetite for roasted sweet potatoes, he's a degenerate."

The Major was about to say something, but looking at his watch he jumped up. "Gracious, Gid, you not only kill your own time but murder mine. It's nearly two o'clock."

"Sit down, John. Don't be snatched."

"Snatched! Wind-bag, you counsel me to blow my life away. Hold your lamp out here so that I can see to get on my horse."

When Gid returned from the passage wherein he had stood to shelter the light, he found Jim on the bench, with no apparent intention of taking his leave; and this he construed to mean that the giant had something on his mind.

"Out with it, Jimmie," he said, as he put the lamp upon the mantel-piece. "I'll sit down here as if it was only early candle-lighting, and let you tell me all about it."

"How do you know I've got anything to say, Uncle Gideon?"

"How do I know when a dog itches? I see him scratch. You have been sitting there in an itching silence and now you begin to scratch. You are more patient than a dog, for you don't scratch until you have itched for some time. Let the fur fly, Jimmie."

Jim laughed, raised his leg and clasped his hands over his knee. "Uncle Gideon, I reckon I'm the happiest man in Cranceford County."

The old man sat leaning back against the wall. His coat was off and under his suspenders he had hooked his thumbs. "Go on, Jimmie; I'm listening."

"She has written another letter—Did Tom tell you anything?" he broke off.

"Did Tom ever tell me anything? Did Tom ever tell anybody anything? Did he ever know anything to tell?"

"She has written another letter and in it she confesses—I don't know how to say it, Uncle Gideon."

"Well, tell me and I'll say it for you. Confesses that she can be happy with no one but you. Go on."

"Who told you? Did Mrs. Cranceford?"

"My dear boy, did Mrs. Cranceford ever tell me anything except to keep off the grass? Nobody has told me anything. Confesses that you are the only man that can make her happy. Now shoot your dye-stuff."

"But that's all there is. She says that her heart will never have a home until my love builds a mansion for it."

"Jimmie, if the highest market price for a fool was one hundred dollars, you'd fetch two hundred."

"Why? Because I believe her when she talks that way—when she gives me to understand that she loves me?"

"No; but because you didn't believe all along that she loved you."

"How could I when she refused to marry me and married another man?"

"That marriage is explained. You've seen the letter she wrote the night before she went away, haven't you?"

"Yes, her mother showed it to me."

"I didn't read it," said Gid, "but the Major gave me the points, and I know that she married that fellow believing that she was saving his soul."

"Yes, I read that," said Jim, "but I didn't know whether she meant it or not. I reckon I was afraid to believe it."

"Well, I know it to be a fact—know it because I know her nature. She's just crank enough—"

"Don't say that," Jim protested, unclasping his hands from his knee and straightening up. "Don't call her a crank when she's an angel."

"That's all right, my dear boy, but heaven is full of the right sort of cranks. Who serves God deeper than the religious crank, and if he's not to be rewarded, who is? By crank I don't mean a weak-minded person; I come nearer meaning a genius."

"I reckon you mean all right," the giant agreed; and after pondering in silence he asked: "Do you reckon she would marry me?"

"I know it. And why not? You are a gentleman and a devilish good-looking fellow. Why, any woman interested in a fine stock show would be proud of you."

At this the giant rubbed his hands together and softly chuckled; but sobering, he said that he could never hope to equal her in thought and quickness of expression, though by reading he would make an effort to attain that end.

"Don't worry about that, Jimmie; and don't you fool yourself that books are everything. They smooth knots, but they don't make timber. Oh, you are smart enough—for a woman."

"I'm not an idiot," said the giant. "Sometimes I can talk without any trouble, and then again I can't say a thing. It's different with you."

The old man's egotism awoke—it never more than dozed. "Jimmie," said he, "it is violating no compact to tell you that I'm no common man. Other men have a similar opinion of themselves and are afraid to spit it out, but I'm bold as well as wise. I know that my opinion doesn't go for much, for I'm too good-humored, too approachable. The blitheness of my nature invites familiarity. You go to a house and make too much of the children, and the first thing you know they'll want to wallow on you all the time. Well, I have made too much of the children of the world, and they wallow on me. But I pinch them sometimes and laugh to hear them squeal. There's only one person that I'm afraid of—Mrs. Cranceford. She chills me and keeps me on the frozen dodge. I always feel that she is reading me, and that makes me more of a rascal—trying to give her something that she can't read.

Look here, if we expect to get any sleep we'd better be at it."

"You go to bed, Uncle Gideon; I'm going to sit up."

"All right; sit there as long as you please." The old fellow got up, and walking stiffly went to the window, drew aside the red calico curtain and looked out. "Don't see much promise of a clear-up," he said. "Not a star in sight. I always dread the rainy season; it makes people look sad, and I want to see them bright—I am most agreeable to them when they're bright. Still, I understand that nothing is more tiresome than eternal sunshine. I wonder if I locked the smokehouse," he went on, turning from the window. "But, come to think, I don't believe I've locked it since about a week ago, when some rascal slipped in and stole nearly all my hams and a bushel of meal. I gad, my old joints work like rusty hinges. Well, I'll lie down now. Good night, Jimmie. Don't slip off before breakfast."

The giant did not hear him. He sat leaning forward, gazing at the cliffs, the mountains, the valleys in the fire. The rain had ceased, but now and then came a dashing shower, like a scouting party, a guerrilla band sweeping through the dark. To the muser there was no time; time had dribbled out and reverie had taken its place. The fire was dying. He saw the red cliffs grow gray along the edges, age creeping over the rocks; he saw a mountain fall into a whitening valley, and he looked up. It was daylight. He went to the door and looked out, and far across the river the brilliant morning sun was rising from a bath of steam.

"You here yet, Jimmie?" The bed loudly creaked, and the giant, looking about, found old Gid sitting on the edge of his couch, rubbing his eyes. "Don't go, for we'll have breakfast now in a minute. I am always glad to look up and find a picture of manliness and strength. It takes me back to my own early days, when I didn't know the meaning of weakness. But I know now—I can feel it all over me. I do think I can dream more foolish things during three to half a dozen winks of sleep than any man that ever lived. Now, what could have put it into my mind to dream that I was born with one leg and was trying at a county fair to swap it off for two? Well, I hear the old woman setting the table out there. Wait till I jump into my clothes and I'll pour a gourd of water for you to wash your face and hands. Had a wash-basin round here somewhere, but don't know what became of it. Had intended to get another, but have been so busy. But I'll tell you there's nothing like a good wash under a pouring gourd. How's your appetite this morning?"

"I don't know."

"Well, you may find it when you sniff old Liza's corn cakes. Now what the deuce became of that other suspender? We used to call them galluses in my day. And now where is that infernal gallus? Beats anything I ever saw in my life. Ah, there it is, over by the window. But how it could have jumped off I don't know. Now let me shove into my old shoes and I'll be with you."

Out in the yard, in a fabulous net of gilded mist they stood, to bathe under the spouting gourd, the mingling of a new day's poetry and the shiftlessness of an old man. "Stream of silver in the gold of a resurrected sun," he said, bareheaded and blinking. "Who'd want a wash-pan? I gad, Jimmie, folks are forgetting how to live. They are putting too much weight on what they can buy for money, unmindful of the fact that the best things of this life are free. Look at that gourd, old, with a sewed-up crack in it, and yet to my mind it serves its purpose better than a china basin. Well, let's go in now and eat a bite. I'm always hungry of a morning. An old fellow is nearer a boy when he first gets up, you know; but he grows old mighty fast after he's had breakfast."

The giant, saying never a word, followed him, the loose boards of the passageway between the two sections of the house creaking and groaning as he trod upon them; and coming to the door he had to stoop, so low had it been cut.

"That's right, Jimmie, duck or you'll lay yourself out. I gad, the world's full of traps set for big fellows. Now sit down there and fall to. Don't feel very brash this morning, do you?"

"I feel first-rate," Jim answered, sitting down.

"Youth and love mixed," said the old man, placing himself at the head of the board. "And ah, Lord, when we grow out of one and forget the other, there's not much left to live for. I'd rather be a young fellow in love than to be an emperor. Help yourself to a slab of that fried ham. She'll bring the coffee pretty soon. Here she comes now. Waiting for you, Aunt Liza. Have some hoe-cake, Jimmie. Yes, sir; youth and love constitute the world, and all that follows is a mere makeshift. Thought may come, but thought, after all, is but a dull compromise, Jimmie, a cold potato instead of a hot roll. Love is noon, and wisdom at its best is only evening. There are some quince preserves in that jar. Help yourself. Thought about her all night, didn't you?"

"I think about her all the time, Uncle Gideon."

"And Jimmie, it wouldn't surprise me if the world should think about her after a while. That woman's a genius."

"I hope not," the giant replied, looking up, and in his voice was a note of distress, and in his eyes lay the shadow of a fear.

"And why not, Jimmie?"

"Because if she should turn out to be a genius she won't marry me."

"That's where your perception is broken off at the end, Jimmie. In the matter of marriage genius is mighty skittish of genius—it seeks the constancy of the sturdy and commonplace. I'll try a dip of those preserves. Now let me see. After breakfast you'd better lie down on my bed and take a nap."

"No, I must go. The Major is going over to Brantly to-day and I want him to bring me a box of cartridges. I forgot to tell him last night."

"Oh, you're thinking about Mayo, eh?"

"Well, I don't know but he did cross my mind. It occurred to me that he might waylay me some night, and I don't want to stand out in the road and dance while he's shooting at me."

"That's right," said the old man. "A fellow cuts a mighty sorry figure dancing under such circumstances. I've tried it."

He shoved his chair back from the table and Jim got up to take his leave. "Look out for the door, Jimmie. Duck as you go under or it will lay you out. Traps set all through life for fellows of your size."

Jim was not oppressed with weariness as he strode along the highway, for in the crisp air a tonic was borne, but loss of sleep had made his senses dreamy, and all things about him were touched with the spirit of unreality—the dead leaves fluttering on the underbrush, the purple mist rising from the fields, the water-mirrors flashing in the road; and so surrendered was he to a listless brooding, forgetful even that he moved along, that he did not notice, up the road, a man leap aside into the woods. The man hid behind a tree, with his eye on the giant and with the barrel of a pistol pressed hard against the bark. Jim passed on, with his hands in his pockets, looking down; and when a clump of bushes, red with frost-dyed leaves, hid him from view, Mayo came out from behind the tree and resumed his journey down the road.

The Major had mounted his horse at the gate and was on the point of riding forth when Jim came up. "Why, good-morning, James," the old gentleman heartily greeted him. "Have you just crawled out of that old man's kennel? I see that the old owl must have kept you up all night. Why, sir, if I were to listen to him I'd never get another wink of sleep."

"I kept myself up," said the giant; and then he added: "I wanted to see you this morning, not very bad, but just to ask you to get me a box of forty-fours when you go to Brantly to-day."

"I'm glad to find you so thoughtful," said the Major. "And I want to tell you right now that you've got to look out for yourself. But staying up all night is no way to begin. Go on into Tom's room and take a nap."

The Major whistled as he rode along, not for want of serious reflection, for he could easily have reached out and drawn in trouble, but because the sharp air stirred his spirits. Nowhere was there a cloud—a speckless day in the middle of a week that had threatened to keep the sky besmirched. Roving bands of negro boys were hunting rabbits in the fields, with dogs that leaped high in low places where dead weeds stood brittle. The pop-eyed hare was startled from his bed among brambly vines, and fierce shouts arose like the remembered yell of a Confederate troop. The holidays were near, the crops were gathered, the winter's wood was up, the hunting season open, but no negro fired a gun. At this time of the year steamboatmen and tavern-keepers in the villages were wont to look to Titus, Eli, Pompey, Sam, Caesar and Bill for their game, and it was not an unusual sight to see them come loaded down with rabbits and quails caught in traps, but now they sat sullen over the fire by day, but were often met prowling about at night. This crossed the Major's mind and drove away his cheerful whistling; and he was deeply thinking when someone riding in haste reined in a horse abreast of him. Looking up he recognized the priest.

"Why, good morning, Mr. Brennon; how are you?"

"Well, I thank you. How far do you go?"

"To Brantly."

"That's fortunate," said the priest, "for I am selfish enough to let you shorten the journey for me."

"I can't do that," the Major laughed, "but we can divide it. I remember overtaking a man one miserable day out in the Indian Territory. He was ignorant, but he was quaint; he couldn't argue, but he could amuse, and he did until he called me a liar, and there our roads split. Don't think, from my telling you this, that I am in the least doubt as to the desirability of your company on the road to Brantly. Been some time since I've seen you, Mr. Brennon."

"Yes; I have been very busy."

"And successfully so, I suppose."

"I am not in a position to complain," said the priest.

"By the way, will you answer a few questions?"

"Gladly, if they're answerable."

"I think they are. Now, the negroes that come into your communion tell you many things, drop idle gossip that may mean much. Did any of them ever drop a hint of preparations which their brethren may or may not be making to demand some unreasonable concession from the white people of this community?"

"What I have seen I am free to relate to you," the priest answered, "but as to what has been told—well, that is quite another matter. I have seen no preparations, but you doubtless remember a conversation we had some time ago, and on that occasion I think we agreed that we might have trouble sooner or later."

"Yes, we were agreed upon that point," the Major replied, "but neither of us professed to see trouble close at hand. For some time I have heard it rumored that the negroes are meeting at night to drill, but I have paid but little attention, giving them credit for more sense than to believe that their uprising could be more than a short, and, to themselves, a disastrous, struggle; but there is one aspect that impresses me, the fact that they are taking no notice of the coming of Christmas; for when this is the case you must know that the negro's nature must have undergone a complete change. I don't quite understand it. Why, sir, at present they can find no possible excuse for revolt. The crops are gathered and they can make no demand for higher wages; no election is near and they can't claim a political cause for disaffection. If they want better pay for their labor, why didn't they strike in the midst of the cotton-picking? That would have been their time for trouble, if that's what they want."

"Perhaps they hadn't money enough to buy equipment, guns and ammunition," the priest suggested. "Perhaps they needed the money that the gathering of the crops would bring them."

The Major looked at him. "I hadn't thought of that," he said. "But surely the negroes have sense enough to know that the whites would exterminate them within a week."

It was some time before Father Brennon replied. His deliberation led the Major to believe that he would speak from his abundant resources; and the planter listened eagerly with his head turned to one side and with his hand behind his ear. "It is possible," the priest began, "that the negro had been harangued to the conviction that he is to begin a general revolt against capital, that labor organizations everywhere will rise up when they hear that he has been bold enough to fire his gun."

The Major's shoulders stiffened. "Sir, if you have known this, why haven't you as a white man and a Southern gentleman told us of it? Why haven't you warned us?"

The priest smiled. "Your resentment is just," said he. "But the truth is, it was not formulated as an opinion until late last night. I called at your house this morning and was told that you had set out for the county-seat. And I have overtaken you."

The Major reined up his horse. Both horses stopped. "Mr. Brennon, you are a gentleman, sir. My hand."

They shook hands and rode on. The Major was deep in thought. "It has all been brought about by that scoundrel Mayo," he said at last. "He has instilled a most deadly poison into the minds of those people. I will telegraph the governor and request him to send the state militia into this community. The presence of the soldiers will dissolve this threatened outbreak; and by the blood, sir, Mayo shall be convicted of treason against the state and hanged on the public square in Brantly. And that will be an end of it."

The priest said nothing, and after a time the Major asked: "How are you getting on with your work?"

"I am greatly encouraged, and I wish I had more time."

"What do you mean by that?"

"I have told you that the church can save the negro. Do you know a negro named Bob Hackett?"

"Yes; he was a worthless politician, but they tell me that he has withdrawn from active politics and gone to work. What about him?"

"He is now a communicant of the church," the priest answered. "He acknowledges a moral authority; and I make bold to say that should trouble come, he will take no part in it. And I make still bolder to say that the church, the foster mother of the soul of man, can in time smooth all differences and establish peace and brotherly regard between the white man and the negro. The Ethiopian cannot change his skin, but true religion whitens his soul and makes him our brother."

"Your sentiment is good," replied the Major, "but religion must recognize an impossibility. The white man and the negro can never hold each other in brotherly regard. Never."

"Don't say never, Major. Men pass from fixed prejudices; the church is eternal in its purpose. Don't say never."

"Well, then, sir," cried the Major, standing in his stirrups, "I will not say never; I will fix a time, and it shall be when the pyramids, moldered to dust, are blown up and down the valley of the Nile."

He let himself down with a jolt, and onward in silence they rode. And now from a rise of ground the village of Brantly was in sight. The priest halted. "I turn back here," he said.

"Mr. Brennon," the Major replied, "between you and me the question of creed should not arise. You are a white man and a gentleman. My hand, sir."

CHAPTER XXIII

Brantly long ago was a completed town. For the most part it was built of wood, and its appearance of decay was so general and so even as to invite the suspicion that nearly all its building had been erected on the same day. In the center of the town was the public square, and about it were ranged the business houses, and in the midst of it stood the court house with its paint blistered and its boards warping. It was square, with a hall and offices below. Above was the court room, and herein was still heard the dying echo of true oratory. On the top of this building, once the pride of the county, was a frail tower, and in it was a clock, always slow. It was never known to record an hour until that hour had long since been due. Sometimes it would save up its strokes upon the bell until fifty or more were accumulated, and then, in the midst of an intense jury trial, it would slowly turn them loose. A mathematician, a man who kept the dates of late and early frosts, had it in his record that the hammer struck the bell sixty-eight times on the afternoon when John Maffy was sentenced to be hanged, and that the judge had to withhold his awful words until this flood of gathered time was poured out. Once or twice the county court had appropriated money to have the clock brought back within the bounds of reason, but a more pressing need had always served to swallow up the sum thus set aside.

A stone planted at one corner of the public square marked the site of a bit of bloody history. Away back in the fifties a man named Antrem, from New England, came to Brantly and, standing where the stone now stands, made an abolition speech. It was so bold an impudence that the citizens stood agape, scarcely able to believe their ears. At last the passive astonishment was broken by a slave-owner named Peel. He drew two pistols, handed one to the speaker, stepped off and told him to defend himself. The New Englander had nerve. He did defend himself, and with deadly effect. Both men were buried on the public square.

A railway had skipped Brantly by ten long and sandy miles, and a new town springing up about a station on the line—an up-start of yesterday, four-fifths of it being a mere paper town, and the other fifth consisting of cheap and hastily built stores, saloons, boarding houses, a livery stable, a blacksmith shop, and a few roughly constructed dwellings—clamored for the county seat; and until this question was finally settled old Brantly could not look with confidence toward any improvement. Indeed, some of her business men stood ready to desert her in the event that she should be beaten by the new town, and while all were bravely willing to continue the fight against the up-start, every one was slow to hazard his money to improve his home or his place of business. Whenever a young man left Brantly it was predicted that he would come to no good, and always there came a report that he was gambling, or drinking himself to death. The mere fact that he desired to leave the old town was fit proof of his general unworthiness to succeed in life.

The Major rode into town, nodding at the loungers whom he saw on the corners of the streets, and tying his horse to the rack on the square, went straightway to the shop of the only hardware dealer and asked for cartridges.

"My stock is running pretty low," said the dealer, wrapping up the paste-board box. "I've sold more lately than I ever sold in any one season before, and yet there's no game in the market."

The Major whistled. "Who has been buying them?" he asked.

"Come to think of it I have sold the most to a Frenchman named Larnage—lives over on the Potter place, I believe. And that reminds me that I'll have a new lot in to-day, ordered for him."

"Do you know anything about that fellow?" the Major asked.

"Not very much."

"Well, don't let him have another cartridge. Keep all you get. We'll need them to protect life and property."

"What! I don't understand."

"I haven't time to explain now, for I'm reminded that I must go at once to the telegraph office. Come over to the court-house."

The Major sent a dispatch to the governor and then went to the county clerk's office where he found the hardware dealer and a number of men waiting for him. The report that he was charged with serious news was already spread about; and when he entered, the clerk of the county court, an old fellow with an ink-blot on his bald head, came forward with an inquiry as to what had been meant when the Major spoke of the cartridges. The Major explained his cause for alarm. Then followed a brief silence, and then the old fellow who kept the records of the frosts and the clock, spoke up with the assertion that for some time he had expected it. "Billy," he said, speaking to the clerk, "I told you the other day that we were going to have trouble mighty soon. Don't you recollect?"

"Don't believe I do, Uncle Parker."

"But I said so as sure as you are standing there this minute. Let me try a little of your tobacco." The clerk handed him a plug, and biting off a chew, the old man continued: "Yes, sir, I've had it in mind for a long time."

"Everybody has talked more or less about it," said the clerk.

"Oh, I know they have, Billy, but not p'intedly, as I have. Yes, sir, bound to come."

"The thing to do is to over-awe them," said the Major. "I have just telegraphed the governor to send the militia down here. And by the way, that fellow Mayo ought to be arrested without delay. Billy, is the sheriff in his office?"

"No, Major, he's gone down to Sassafras to break up a gang of negro toughs that have opened a gambling den. He'll be back this evening and I'll have the warrant ready for him by the time he gets back. Any of us can swear it out—reckon all our names better go to it."

"Yes," the Major agreed, "we'd better observe the formalities of the law. The militia will undo all that has been done, and as for the fellow that brought about the inquietude, we'll see him hanged in front of this door."

Old man Parker, who kept the records, nudged his neighbor and said: "Inquietude is the word. I told my wife last night, says I, 'Nancy, whenever you want the right word, go to John Cranceford.' That's what I said. Major; and I might have said go to your father if he was alive, for he stood 'way up among the pictures, I tell you; and I reckon I knowd him as well as any man in the county. I ricollect his duel with Dabney."

"He was to have fought a man named Anderson Green," replied the Major, "but a compromise was effected."

"Yes," said Parker, "Green's the man I was tryin' to think of. It was Shelton that fought Dabney."

"Shelton fought Whitesides," said the Major.

The men began to titter, "Well, then, who was it fought Dabney?"

"Never heard of Dabney," the Major answered.

"Well, I have, and somebody fought him, but it makes no difference. So, in your father's case a compromise was effected. The right word again; and that's what makes me say to my wife, 'Nancy, whenever you want the right word go to John Cranceford;' and, as I said a while ago, your father either, for I knowd him as well as any man, and was present at the time he bought a flat-boat nigger named Pratt Boyce."

"My father was once forced to sell, but he never bought a negro," the Major replied.

"That so? Well, now, who was it bought Pratt Boyce? You fellers shut up your snortin'. I reckon I know what I'm talkin' about."

The county judge and several other men came in and the talk concerning the threatened negro outbreak was again taken up. "It seems rather singular," said the Judge, "that we should worry through a storm of politics and escape any very serious bloodshed and reach a climax after all these years. Of course when two races of people, wholly at variance in morals and social standing, inhabit the same community, there is always more or less danger, still I don't think that the negroes have so little sense—"

"Ah, the point I made," the Major broke in. "But you see a labor plank has been added to their platform of grievance."

Parker nudged his neighbor. "I says, says I, 'Nancy, John Cranceford for the right word.'"

"There's something in that," the Judge replied. "Nothing can be madder than misled labor. We have been singularly free from that sort of disturbances, but I suppose our time must come sooner or later. But I think the militia will have a good effect so far as the negroes themselves are concerned. But of course if the soldiers come and the trouble blows over without any demonstration whatever, there will be considerable dissatisfaction among the people as to why such a step should have been taken. Uncle Parker," he added, turning to the record-keeper, "think we'll have much cold weather this winter?"

Parker did not answer at once. He knew that glibness would argue against due meditation. "I see a good many signs," he slowly answered. "Hornets hung their nests on the low limbs of the trees, and there are other indications, still it largely depends on the condition of the wind. Sometimes a change of wind knocks out all calculations, still, I feel assured in saying that we are goin' to have a good deal of frost first and last; but if the militia don't get here in time we are mighty apt to have it hotter before we have it colder. Last night while I sat at home by the fire a smokin' of my pipe, and Nancy a-settin' there a-nittin' a pair of socks for a preacher, I looks up and I says, 'there's goin' to be trouble in this community before many changes of the moon,' I says, and I want at all surprised to-day when the Major here come a-ridin' in with his news. Don't reckon any of you ricollect the time we come mighty nigh havin' a nigger uprisin' before the war. But we nipped it in the bud; and I know they hung a yaller feller that cost me fifteen hundred dollars in gold."

The old man was so pleased to find himself listened to by so large a company that he squared himself for a longer discourse upon happenings antedating the memory of any one present, but attention split off and left him talking to a neighbor, who long ago was weary of the sage's recollections. Wisdom lends its conceit to the aged, and Parker was very old; and when his neighbor gave him but a tired ear, he turned from him and boldly demanded the Major's attention, but at this moment the telegraph operator came in with a dispatch. And now all interests were centered. The Major tore open the envelope and read aloud the following from the governor:

"Troops are at competitive drill in Mississippi. Have ordered them home."

The Major stood leaning with his elbow on the top of the clerk's tall desk. He looked again at the dispatch, reading it to himself, and about him was the sound of shuffling feet.

"Well, it won't take them more than twenty-four hours to get home," he said, "and that will be time enough. But Billy, we'd better not swear out that warrant till they come."

"That's wise," said the Judge, a cautious man. "His followers would not stand to see him taken in by the civil authorities; it's not showy enough."

And Parker, speaking up, declared the Judge was right. "I ricollect the militia come down here once durin' the days of the carpet-baggers, and—"

"But let no one speak of the dispatch having been sent to the governor," said the Judge. "Billy, when the sheriff comes back you'd better tell him to appoint forthwith at least a hundred deputies."

"In fact," the Major replied, "every law-abiding man in the county might be declared a deputy."

Old Parker found his neighbor and nudged him. "I says to my wife, 'Nancy,' says I, 'whenever you want the right idee, go to John Cranceford and you'll get it.'"

"That's all right, Uncle Parker," the irritated man replied. "I don't give a continental and you needn't keep on coming to me with it."

"You don't? Then what sort of a man are you?"

"You boys quit your mowling over there," the county clerk commanded.

"Major," said the Judge, "the troops will doubtless come by boat and land near your place. Don't you think it would be a good idea for you to come over with them? The truth is you know our people are always more or less prejudiced against militia, and it is therefore best to have a well-known citizen come along with them."

"I don't know but that you are right," said the Major. "Yes, I will come with them."

He bade the men good day and turned to go, and out into the hall the Judge came following him. "By the way, Major," said he, "you are of course willing to take all responsibility;

and I'd a little rather you wouldn't mention my name in connection with the militia's coming down here, for the ordering out of troops is always looked upon as a sort of snap judgment."

"I thought you said that you were not going to run for office again," the Major bluntly replied.

The Judge stammered and though the hall was but dimly lighted, the Major saw that his face was growing red.

"I have reconsidered that," confessed the politician, "and next season I shall be a candidate for re-election."

"And I will oppose you, sir."

"Oppose me? And why so?"

"Because you've got no nerve. I believe, sir, that in your smooth way you once took occasion to say that Gideon Batts was a loud-mouth and most imprudent man. But, sir, there is more merit in the loud bark of a dog than in the soft tread of a cat. I will oppose you when the time comes, but I will shoulder the responsibility of martial law in this community. Good day, sir."

"Major—"

"I said good day, sir."

The old gentleman strode hotly out to the rack where his horse was tied, and thereabout was gathered a number of boys, discussing the coming danger which in their shrewdness they had keenly sniffed. Among them he distributed pieces of money, wherewith to buy picture books, he said, but they replied that they were going to buy powder and he smiled upon them as he mounted his horse to ride away.

In the road not far distant from the town he met Larnage, the Frenchman. The day before he would have passed him merely with a nod, as he scarcely knew him by sight and had forgotten his name; but the hardware dealer had recalled it and upon it had put an emphasis; so, reining up his horse, he motioned the man to stop.

"How long have you been in this neighborhood?" the Major asked. At this abruptness the Frenchman was astonished.

"I do not understand," he replied.

"Yes you do. How long have you been here?"

"Oh, I understand that, but I do not understand why you should ask."

"But can't you tell me?"

"I can be so obliging. I have lived here two years."

"And how long in the United States?"

"Ten years. And now will you have the goodness to tell me why you wish to know? Will you be so kind as I have been?"

"Well, to be frank, I don't hear a very good report of you."

"But who is appointed to make a report of me? I attend to my own business, and is this a bad report to make of a citizen of the country? If you will have the goodness to pardon me I will ride on."

"Wait a moment. Why are you buying so many cartridges?"

The Frenchman shrugged his shoulders. "Has not the citizen of the country a right to spend his money? I have heard that the Major is polite. He must not be well to-day. Shall I ride on now? Ah, I thank you."

Onward the Frenchman rode, and gazing back at him the Major mused: "The frog-eater gave me the worst of it. But I believe he's a scoundrel all the same. I didn't get at him in the right way. Sorry I said anything to him."

CHAPTER XXIV

Upon reaching home shortly after nightfall the Major found visitors waiting for him in the library—Wash Sanders, old Gid, Jim Taylor, Low, and a red bewhiskered neighbor named Perdue. A bright fire was crackling in the great fire-place; and with stories of early steamboat days upon the Mississippi, Gid was regaling the company when the hero of the yarn opened the door and looked in. Getting to their feet with a scuffle and a clatter of shovel and tongs (which some one knocked down) they cried him a welcome to his own house.

"Gentlemen," said the Major, "just wait till I eat a bite and I'll be with you. Have you all been to supper?"

"We have all been stuffed," Gid took the liberty to answer, "all but Wash Sanders and he—"

"Don't eat enough to keep a chicken alive," Sanders struck in. "Wish I could eat with you, Major, but I ain't got no relish for vidults. But I'm glad to know that other folks ain't that bad off. Jest go on and take your time like we want here waitin' for you."

While the Major was in the dining-room, Gid came out and told him that the priest had said to him and to others that it might be well to call at the Major's house immediately upon his return from Brantly.

"He's all right," said the Major, getting up and taking the lead toward the library. And when he had sat down in his chair, bottomed with sheep-skin, he told his friends of his fears of a negro insurrection, of the dispatch and of the answer from the governor; and he related his talk with the Frenchman, whereupon Low, the Englishman, spoke up:

"I know that chap. It wouldn't surprise me to learn that he put some rascally black up to the trick of punching that hole in my bath. For a time he came about my place quite a bit, you know, but I gave him to understand one day that I vastly preferred to choose my own associates. And you may rest with the assurance that he will be against the whites. Ah, with a Frenchman it is never a question as to which side he shall take. By jove, he always finds out which side the Englishman is on and then takes the other. I have brought with me a bit of Scotch whisky and I shall be pleased to have you gentlemen join me."

"Wait a minute," said the Major. "I have some liquor that was distilled sixty years ago by the grandfather of the commander of the Alabama. We'll try that first."

"Good!" cried the Briton. "I can't deny the Alabama claim, you know." And then he added: "Most extraordinary, I assure you."

"Just wait till you smack your mouth on it," said Gid. "Why, sir, there's the smile of a goddess in each drop and a 'Paradise Regained' in a swallow. Sit down, Wash Sanders—a swig of it would shoot you into the air like a rocket."

"But really, Mr. Gid, I think a little of it would help my

appetite," Sanders replied, looking anxiously toward the Major.

"Appetite!" Gid cried. "You can eat the hind leg of a rhinoceros right now."

"Do you mean to insult me, sir?" Sanders retorted, weakly bristling up; and the Major turning from the sideboard, with the odd-shaped bottle and several glasses in his hands, looked at Batts and said: "Don't, Gid."

"All right, but I was joking," the old rascal declared. "Wash and I always prank with each other. You can take a joke, can't you, Wash?"

"With the best of them," Sanders answered. "Yes, sir, and before the doctors proved to me that I couldn't get well I was joking all the time." He raised his hand and with his long finger nail scratched his chin. "But they showed me that I couldn't get well and if that ain't enough to sadden a man's life I don't know what is."

"Now, gentlemen," said the Major, "I want you to help yourselves, and not be afraid, for the glasses are shallow and the bottle is deep."

The red bewhiskered man Perdue, who had said nothing, took out his quid of tobacco and with a loud "spat," threw it against the chimney-back. "I'll join you," he said, grinning. "Never saw any liquor too old for me."

They stood and touched glasses. Gid walled his eyes like a steer, and with a rub of his breast and an "ah-hah," he nodded at Low. "What do you think of that?" he cried. "Isn't it a miracle?"

"Ah, it is very smooth," Low answered, sipping. "Most uncommon I should think."

"Smooth," said Gid. "Did you say smooth? It is as silk woven in the loom of a dream. Wash, how does it strike you?"

"I think it will help me," Sanders answered.

"Help you!" And under his breath Gid added: "Ought to kill you."

"What did you say?" Sanders asked.

"Said it wouldn't kill you."

"Oh, I think not. Really, after a while I might be tempted to go out and eat something. How are you gettin' along, Perdue?"

"Shakin' hands with my grandfather in the speret," Perdue declared, and running his fingers through his fiery whiskers he laughed with a hack that cut like the bleat of a sheep.

"Jim," said the Major, turning to Taylor, who had not left his seat, "you'd better try a little. It won't hurt you."

"No, thank you, Major, I'm afraid of it."

"Let him alone," Gid spoke. "One drink of this and he'd carry off the gate, posts and all and leave them on the hill. Don't tempt him."

"Gentlemen," said Perdue, "I have always made it a rule never to repeat anything that my children say, for I know how such a thing bores folks, but I will tell you what my son

Ab said the other night. His mother was gettin' him ready for bed—just a little more, Major. There, that's a plenty. Mother was gettin' him ready for bed and he looked up—"

"I feel the blood of youth mounting from the feet of the past to the head of the present," Gid broke in. "I can jump a ten rail fence, staked and ridered."

"And I'm pretty jumpy myself," the Major declared. "But what were you going to say, Perdue?"

"I was goin' to say that I always make it a rule never to repeat anything that my children say, for I have often had fellers bore me with the smart sayin's of their children—and I know that most every man thinks that his children are the brightest in the country and all that—but the other night as my wife was gettin' Ab ready for bed he looked up—"

"We never had any children at our house," said Wash Sanders, scratching his chin with his polished finger-nail, "but I jest as good as raised one nephew. You remember Dan, don't you, Major?"

"Mighty well. Went to Texas, didn't he?"

"Yes, and got to cowboyin' around and was killed."

"I recall that he was a very bright young man," said the Major. "But what were you going to say, Perdue?"

"I was goin' to say that I always make it a rule never to tell anything that my children say, knowin' how it seems to pester folks, for I have been nearly bored to death by fellers breakin' in and tellin' what they of course thought was a powerful smart thing, said by one of their children—so I am mighty keerful about such things, makin' it a rule never to repeat anything said by my children, but the other night as my wife was gettin' Ab ready for bed—"

"Somebody's hollering helloa at the gate," said Jim. "Hush a minute. There it is again."

The Major went out and presently returned, bringing with him a large blue envelope. "It's from the county clerk," he said, sitting down and breaking the seal. "Brought by a deputy sheriff, and he said that he had ridden hard all the way and was in a great hurry to get back. Let's see what old Billy has to say." And now having put on his spectacles, he read aloud the following:

> "Marcus T. Berry, sheriff of this the county of Cranceford, in the State of Arkansas, did on this day seek to break up a den of negro gamblers at Sassafras, in the before mentioned county of Cranceford, and State as above set forth, and while in the discharge of his duty, was then and there fired upon and so desperately wounded that in his home in the town of Brantly, seat of the said county of Cranceford, State as before mentioned, he now lies at the point of death. The negroes claimed that they were not gambling, but engaged in lawful merchandise; but be that as it may, the sheriff and his posse were there and then fired upon, and besides the wounding of the sheriff, two men were killed outright, to-wit, one James Mattox and one Leon Smyers, and the same were left there. The sheriff managed to make his escape, albeit he was followed and repeatedly fired upon. And be it known that the report now reaches here that the atrocity did not cease with the firing on of the sheriff's posse, but that a sharp fight afterward took place between negroes and white men near by; and we are now informed that a strong force of negroes, at the instance of one Mayo, is now gathering in the southwestern part of the

county, preparatory to a march upon this, the seat of the county of Cranceford. Therefore, it behooves all good citizens to meet in the before mentioned town for the defense of life and property, as it is here that the blow is to fall.

William N. Haines,

Clerk of the County of Cranceford, in the State of Arkansas."

Scarcely observing a pause the Major had read the letter, and no word of surprise had been spoken by his listeners; and now in silence they looked at one another, Gid with his mouth open, Sanders with an expression of pain.

"Well," said the Major, "that settles it."

"By jove," the Englishman burst out, "I should rather say unsettles it. I can't conceive of a settlement on that basis, you know. Those blacks are positively annoying. First they punch a hole in my bath and then they fire on a sheriff's party. I should call it a most extraordinary approach toward the settlement of a difficult problem. But now, gentlemen, if you'll join me we'll take a bit of Scotch whisky."

Old Gid looked hard at him. "What?" said he, "insult old Semmes' liquid music with a hot breath of peat smoke! Never, sir. And consequently I'll take another glimpse at this mountain sunrise."

The Englishman laughed. "You have a most extraordinary way of boasting, you know. You may take your sunrise on the mountain, but I prefer this moonlight in the heather. A glass about half full of water, please. Thank you, very kind I assure you." The Briton sat and sipped his Scotch while the

Major paced up and down the room, hands behind him, deep in thought. But soon he took his chair again, a proof that what now was to come was not a speculation but the outline of a plan of action.

"Where's Tom?" he asked, nodding at Gid, but with an eye upon Wash Sanders.

"Over at my house," Wash Sanders answered.

"Well, when you go home, take this message to him. Say that I said go at once to the neighbors for five miles below your house, along the county road, and tell them that trouble of a serious nature has come—tell them to meet, men, women and children, at my house by daylight in the morning. Have him remind them that his house, on account of its situation high above the river, is the easiest to defend, and that it will accommodate more people than any other house in the neighborhood. Tell the men, of course, to bring their arms and all the ammunition they have. Explain that a sufficient number of men will be left here to protect the women and children, while the large majority of us will make all possible haste to the county seat. Tell the men to come mounted. Now is it clear to you?"

"Major," Wash Sanders spoke up with more than his usual show of spirit, "the doctors have condemned my body but they hain't condemned my mind. It is clear to me, sir, and I will go now."

"All right," said the Major. "And Jim," he added, "you do the same with the upper end of the road."

The giant was smoking. He stood his pipe against a corner of the fire-place, got up and without saying a word, strode away. Wash Sanders was soon gone, after halting at the door to say that he might not be able to eat enough to keep a setting hen alive, but that he reckoned he could pull a trigger with any man that ever came over the pike. And now the Major, old Gid and the Englishman sat looking into the fire.

"War time, Gid," said the Major.

"Yes, without banners and without glory," the old fellow replied.

"You are right. In the opinion of the majority of Americans, bravery on our part will be set down as a cruelty and a disgrace. The newspaper press of the north will condemn us. But we can't help that, for a man must protect his home. Mr. Low, there is nothing so unjust as politics."

"We have had many examples of it in England, sir."

"Yes," said the Major, "there have been examples of it everywhere. In this country political influences have narrowed some of the broadest minds."

"In England political prejudices have killed poets," the Englishman said.

"And now," Gid put in, "while you are discussing the evil I will try a little more of the good. John, have another peep at the blue dome above?"

"No, I must go and give Mrs. Cranceford old Billy's letter."

"Won't it alarm her?" the Englishman asked.

"Oh, not in the least," the Major answered, and old Gid smiled. "You couldn't scare her with a bell-mouth blunderbuss," he declared.

The Major now had reached the door, but turning back he said: "You gentlemen better sleep here to-night."

In a state of apparent alarm the Englishman sprang to his feet. "My bath," he cried. "No, I can't stop. I must have my bath."

"But you can bathe here."

"Oh, no, I must have my own tub, you know. But I shall be here early at morning. I must go now. Good night," he added, reaching the door. "You are very kind, I assure you." And when thus he had taken his leave, the Major, pointing at a lamp, said to Gid: "End room down the porch. Go to bed."

CHAPTER XXV

Early at morning, just as the dawn began to pale the sandy bluffs along the shore, and while the cypress bottoms still lay under the blackness of night, there came the trampling of horses, the low tones of men, the sharp, nervous voices of women, and the cries of children untimely gathered from their trundle-beds. The Major and his wife were ready to receive this overflow of company. A spliced table was stretched nearly the full length of the long hall, and a great kettle of coffee was blubbering on the fire. There were but three negroes on the place, one man and two women—the others had answered a call at midnight and had gone away. But the remaining ones were faithful; at a drowsy hour they left their beds and with no word of complaint took it upon themselves to execute a new and hurried task. "Bill," said the Major, "I want you and your wife and Polly to understand that I never forget such faithfulness as you are now showing, and when I come back—but now is the best time. Here are ten dollars apiece for you and you must remember that as long as I live you shall never want for anything."

Fifty men arrived before the east was flushed with the sun. It was decided that ten of these, including Wash Sanders, should be left to protect the women and children. The least active were chosen. All but the younger ones had followed Lee through the dark days of his last campaign. The Major took command and martial law prevailed. He buckled on no sword but he looked like a soldier; and short, sharp sentences that he had forgotten at the close of the war now came back to him.

"Make ready, men. Time passes. Mount."

There were pale faces in the hall and at the gate where the men sat their horses, ready to ride, but there was bravery and no tears. The command was drawn up; the Major, not yet mounted, stood talking to Wash Sanders, when suddenly down the road a chant arose. All eyes were turned that way, and strange to them was the sight they beheld—the Catholic priest, with slow and solemn pace, treading the middle of the road, holding high aloft a black crucifix; and behind him followed the negro members of his church, men, women and children. He was leading his people to the hills—out of danger. As the head of this weird procession came opposite the gate, where now the Major stood with folded arms, the priest gravely smiled and higher held his crucifix. And then, silently, and looking neither to the right nor to the left, came out the three negroes who had remained at home; and taking up the chant they joined their brothers and sisters. They marched solemnly onward, turned into a road that led to the hills, the wind hushing their chant, but the black cross still seen high above their dusky, upturned faces. For full five minutes the Major stood in silence, gazing, and then hastily mounting, he shouted: "Forward!" and his troop swept down the road. He chose the nearest course and it lay by the old house wherein Louise had lived; and again he heard the wind moaning in the ragged plum thicket.

Along the road the scattered houses were deserted, and in many a cabin the fire-place was cold, and many a door stood open. Not a negro was seen—yes, one, an old man drawn with rheumatism, sitting on a bench, waiting for the sun to warm his joints.

When the Major and his troop rode into the town they found it quiet—under the weight of a heavy dread. They were looked upon from windows, where men were posted, waiting; and obeying a shouted instruction, the Major led his men to a long, low shed not far from the scene of expected blood-flow, to stable their horses. Following them came old Billy, the county clerk; and when the horses had been put away, he came up and thus addressed the Major:

"You are to take command."

"All right. What has been done?"

"Not much of anything. Nothing could be done except to wait."

"How many men have we?"

"It is surprising how few," old Billy answered. "We didn't realize how weak the white population was until danger came. We have about three hundred, and more than a thousand negroes are marching on the town. We held a sort of council this morning and agreed that we'd better post as many as we can in the court-house. It commands all the streets and besides we must save the records."

They were now marching toward the court-house. "Where are the women and children?" the Major inquired.

"In the brick warehouse with a force of men near."

"Well, I suppose you've done all you can. It would be nonsense to engage them in the open, but with our men posted about the square not more than two-thirds of them can get action at once. Those poor devils are as well armed as we and are wrought upon by fanaticism. It is going to be desperate for a time. At first they'll be furious. Has any one heard of Mayo?"

"He's at their head and the Frenchman is with him."

"How is the sheriff?"

"Dead."

They filed into the court-house, where a number of men were already gathered, posted above and below. "Bring an axe and cut loop-holes," the Major commanded. "When the fight begins you can't very well fire from the windows. How are you, Uncle Parker?"

"Able to be about, Major. You wan't old enough for the Mexican War, was you? No, of course not. But I was there and this here fightin' agin such odds puts me in mind of it."

"Good morning, Major." It was the voice of the County Judge.

"Good morning, sir. I see you have a gun. Don't you think it impolitic? But pardon me. This is no time for ill-humored banter."

The Judge bowed. "Now I recall John Cranceford, the soldier," said he. "This is a great pity that has come upon us, Major," he added.

"Worse than that," the Major replied. "It is a curse. The first man who landed a slave in America ought to have been hanged."

"And what about the men who freed them?"

"They were American soldiers, sir, as brave a body of men as ever trod the face of the earth. Captain Batts, what are you trying to do there?"

"Thought I'd take a nap," old Gid answered. "You can wake me up when the fight begins—don't want to miss it."

"If you go to sleep I will court-martial you, sir. Superintend the cutting of the loop-holes."

"All right, don't believe I'm very sleepy anyway;" and as he shuffled away the Englishman turned to the Major and asked:

"And is he game, sir?"

"As a lion," the Major answered.

"But he blows, you know," said the Englishman.

"And so does a lion roar, sir," the Major rejoined.

The Major inspected the other posts, to the right and left of the square, and then took active command of the lower floor of the court-house; and when the holes had been cut Gid was told to command the floor above. Tom Cranceford was ordered to serve on the floor above. At this he began to grumble, pouting that he couldn't be in the rush if one should come; but the Major stormed at him. "It is more dangerous up there if that's what you want, and I'll be with you now and then to see that you are kept busy. March this instant or I'll drive you to home duty under Wash Sanders."

From the windows and the loop-holes guns could be seen

bristling everywhere, and the minutes that passed were slow and weary with waiting. Directly across from the court-house was a broad and low brick store house, with but a single window above, facing the square; and the Major looking at it for a time, turned to the old clerk and said: "That building is the strongest one in town, but no men appear to be posted in it. Why so?"

"The rear wall is torn out and the men would be unprotected from behind," the clerk answered. "The wall was pulled down about a month ago. Evans was going to have the house built deeper into the lot so he could use it as a cotton shed, but hasn't."

"Bad that it was left that way. How long since the last scout came in?"

"About an hour and a half."

"And where was the enemy then?"

"In the neighborhood of Gum Springs."

"That's bad. The militia won't have time to get here."

The Major went above, where he found Gid's men posted at the windows and the loop-holes. "How is everything?" he asked.

"Lovely, John."

"Don't call me John."

"All is well, Major."

"Good." And after a time he added: "The south road is so

crooked that we don't command it very far, therefore look sharp. Back to your post!" he stormed as Perdue looked up from his loop-hole. "This is no time for idleness."

"I wonder what time we eat," said Gid.

"You may never eat another bite," the Major answered.

"Then I don't reckon there's any use to worry about it, John, or Major, I mean."

The Major returned to the floor below. "This is getting to be quite a lark," said the Englishman. "It's beastly cruel to fight, but after all it is rather jolly, you know."

"I'm glad you think so, sir; I can't," the Major replied. "I regard it as one of the worst calamities that ever befell this country."

"Do you think there will be much pillage by the blacks—much burning of houses?"

"Possibly, but to sustain their cause their commander will hold them in some sort of check. He is looking out for the opinion of labor unions, the scoundrel. He is too sharp to give his war a political cast."

"Ah, but to butcher is a beastly way to look after good opinion. What's that?" the Englishman cried.

From afar, through the stillness that lay along the south road, came the popping of rifles; and then all was still. Then came the sounds of hoofs, and then a riderless horse dashed across the square.

"Steady, men, they are upon us!" the Major shouted, and

then all again was still. From the windows nothing could be seen down the road, and yet the advance guard must be near, for a gun was fired much closer than before. Now upon the square a rider dashed, and waving his hat he cried: "They are coming through the fields!" He dismounted, struck his horse with his hat to drive him out of danger and ran into the court-house. The Major met him. "They will be here in no time," the man said. "But how they got so close without my seeing them is a mystery to me. But of course I expected to see them in the road and didn't look for them in the fields. And that ain't all. They've got a cannon."

"What!" the Major exclaimed, and the men at the loop-holes looked back at him.

"Yes," the scout went on, "and I know all about it. Just before the war ended an enormous gun was spiked, dismantled and thrown into a well way down on the Dinkler place. It was got out a good while afterward and the spike drilled out, and since then it has been used for a Christmas gun. Well, they've got that thing on an ox wagon, but they've got no way to fire it for—"

The guns to the right and left of the square blurted out, then came a roar and a yell, and in an instant the opposite side of the square was black with negroes pouring out from behind the low brick building. With a howl and a rush they came, but from three sides volley after volley was poured into them, the white men using their shot guns. The effect was terrible, and soon the square was cleared of all but the dead and the wounded. A cessation fell, and Mayo's voice could be heard, shouting at his men. He saw that to attempt to take the house by storm was certain death, so to comparative safety behind the house and into a deep-cut road a little farther back he withdrew his men. He had not expected so early to find such opposition, and his aim was to crush with the senseless weight of force, but the shot-guns were too deadly. Now he was cool and cautious. The fire from the whites was straggling. Suddenly out from behind the brick building rushed three black giants, torches in hand, making desperately for the court-house. It was indeed a forlorn hope, for one by one they fell, the last, so death-defying was he, that he fell upon the steps and his torch flew from his hand into the hallway and crackled on the floor. A man reached out to grasp it, but a shattered arm was drawn back. "Not you, Major!" cried old Parker. Outward he leaned, grabbing at the torch, but Mayo's guns swept the hall. And when they drew the old man back, he brought the snapping pine, but left his life. They laid him out upon the floor, stood for a moment sadly to view him; and through a hole a bullet zipped and beside him fell a neighbor.

"Back to your places!" the Major commanded. Now the guns on the opposite side of the square were silent. "They are lying low and our men can't reach them," said the Major. "What are they up to now? Preparing for another charge?"

"Worse than that," said the man who had seen them in the fields. "They have hoisted that cannon up into the brick building and are going to poke it through the window. See there! See that big log up-ended? That's to brace it. From where I lay I saw them just now breaking up an old stove out in the lot and they are going to load with the fragments. I killed two of them, but they got the stove away. Listen, don't you hear them pounding it up?"

"And this house will afford no more protection that so much paper," said the Major, speaking low. "We have badly planned our defense. We are ill protected from bullets, and a cannon will blow us into the air." And then, moving from one to another, he looked through the loop-holes. "Train every gun on that window," he commanded, "and shoot if a finger is seen." Up the stairs he bounded. Old Gid was walking up and down the room, softly whistling. "Pretty peppery, Major," he said, pointing to three bodies stretched upon the floor.

"Yes," the Major replied, "and it will be worse. We are doomed."

"How so? Keep on rushing till they wear us out? I reckon not. It would take five thousand men. God, but look at them lying out there. They were desperate, but they are toned down."

"They've got a cannon loaded with the fragments of a stove and will fire it from that window," said the Major.

Gid whistled and resumed his walk. The firing about the square was slow and steady. From across the way there came no gun shot. "Got a cannon, eh?" old Gid mused. "I wondered why they were so still," and then to the Major he said: "They'll shell us out and mow us down at their leisure. Who built this infernal court-house?"

"I don't remember," the Major answered, "but he ought to be in here now. Train your guns on that window."

The Major went below. Just as he reached the bottom of the stairway he leaped forward with a cry. He saw Jim Taylor jump from a window out upon the square. The Major ran to a loop-hole, pushed a man aside and looked out. And now there was a belching of guns on the other side. Jim Taylor caught up a child in his arms, and with bullets pecking up the dirt about him and zipping against the wall, he dodged behind a corner of the house. Then he ran across the protected side of the square. Near by, in the door of a warehouse, a woman stood, shrieking. When she saw the giant with her little boy in his arms she ran out to meet him, breaking loose from the hands that strove to hold her, and snatching the little fellow, she cried: "God bless you for this. I have so many little ones to see to that he got out and went to look for his grandpa Parker. God bless you, sir."

The giant had seen old Parker lying dead on the floor, but he said nothing; he turned about, and entering the court-house from the protected side, was soon at his post. The Major stormed at him. "You've lost all your sense," he cried. "You are a bull-calf, sir. Now see that you don't leave your post again. Did they hit you?" he anxiously asked.

"Don't believe they did," the giant grimly answered.

"Well, they will in a minute. Look there!"

The mouth of the cannon showed above the window, shoved through and now rested on the ledge; and behind it arose an enormous log. From the loop-holes in the court-house the gun was raked with buck-shot, but all the work was done from below and no one stood exposed. Once a hand, like a black bat, was seen upon the gun, but instantly it flew away, leaving a blotch of blood. And now the old bell, so quiet all the morning, began to strike—one, two, ten, thirty—slowly, with dread and solemn pauses.

"Look!" the Major cried. A red-hot poker glowed above the cannon. Buckshot hailed from a hundred guns, and the poker fell, but soon it came again and this time flat upon the gun. The hand that held it was nervous and fumbling. Suddenly the breech of the gun slipped lower down the upright log. Up went the muzzle, and then came a deafening boom. There was a crash over-head. The cupola of the court-house was shattered, and down came the bell upon the roof, and off it rolled and fell upon the ground with a clang. Out surged

Mayo's men, but a fearful volley met them, and amid loud cries and with stumbling over the dead and the dying, torn and bleeding, they were driven back. But they set up a yell when they saw the damage their gun had wrought. They could foresee the havoc of a better managed fire. Now the yells were hushed. The Major's men could hear a black Vulcan hammering his iron; then a lesser noise—they were driving the scraps into the gun.

"It will be worse this time," said the Major. "They have cut a deeper niche in the log to hold the breech and there'll be no chance of its slipping. These walls will be shattered like an eggshell. Steady, they are at it."

Again the gun lay across the window ledge. The red-hot poker bobbed up, glowing in the dim light, but there was a crash and a rain of shot and it flew back out of sight; and it must have been hurled through the rear opening of the wall, for they were a long time in getting it. But it came again, this time sparkling with white heat. The guns about the square kept up an incessant fire, but over the powder the poker bobbed, and then—the whole town shook with the terrific jar, and windows showered their glass upon the street, and through the smoke a thrilling sight was seen—the roof of the brick building was blown into splinters and in the air flew boots, hats and the fragments of men—the gun had exploded.

"Out and charge!" the Major shouted. "Forward, Captain Batts!" he cried at the foot of the stairs, and the men came leaping down. The cry was taken up, and from every building about the square the men were pouring. Mayo had no time to rally his force; indeed, it was beyond his power, for his men were panic-smitten. Into the fields and toward the woods they ran for their lives. It was now a chase. Bang, to right and the left, and in the fields the fleeing blacks were falling, one by one. Once or twice they strove to make a stand, but hell snorted in their faces—and death barked at their heels. In their terror they were swift, but from afar the rifles sucked their blood. The woods were gained and now they were better protected in their flight, dodging from tree to tree; some of them faced about and white men fell, and thus was caution forced upon the pursuers. So much time was gained that Mayo rallied the most of his men, but not to stand and fight. He had another plan. In a small open space, once a cotton patch, stood a large church, built of logs, and thither he hastened his men, and therein they found a fortress. The Major called in his scattered forces. They gathered in the woods about the church.

"Are you going to charge them?" old Gideon asked.

"No, sir, that would be certain death to many of us. Hemmed in as they now are they'll be deadly desperate. We'll have to manage it some other way." A shower of buck-shot flew from the church.

"I gad, Major, they've got buck-shot," said Gid. "And they could mow us down before we could cross that place. They still outnumber us two to one—packed in there like sardines. Don't you think we'd better scatter about and peck at 'em when they show an eye? I'd like to know who built that church. Confound him, he cut out too many windows to suit me."

"Dodge down, men!" cried the Major. "Mr. Low, get back there, sir!"

"Be so kind as to oblige me with the time," said Low. "The rascals have smashed my watch. Punch a hole in my bath and then ruin my watch, you know. Most extraordinary impudence, I assure you."

"It is half-past three," said the Major. "And what a day it has been and it is not done yet."

Jim Taylor came forward. "Look out," said the Major. "They'll get you the first thing you know. Why don't you pick up a few grains of sense as you go along?"

"Why don't some one scatter a few grains?"

"Hush, sir. I want no back talk from you."

"But I've got an idea," said the giant, with a broad grin.

"Out with it."

"Why, right over yonder is the Nelson plantation storehouse," said Jim, "and at the front end is the biggest door I ever saw, double oak and so thickly studded with wrought-iron nails that their broad heads touch. And my idea is this: Take that door, cut a round hole in the center with a cold-chisel, cut down a good-sized cypress tree, round off one end, fit it in the hole, with about five feet sticking through; let a lot of us strong fellows gather up the tree and, protected by the door, use it for a battering ram and punch that house down. Then we can work them freely, as the fellow says."

"Jim," the Major cried, "you are learning something. This day has developed you. I believe that can be done. At least it is worth trying. But, men, if it should be effective, let there be as little unnecessary slaughter as possible. We are compelled to kill—well, we can't help it. However, take Mayo alive if you possibly can. I want to see him hanged on the public square. Now get the door. Here, Tom, you and Low cut down a cypress tree. Here, Lacy, you help. Low doesn't know how to handle an ax. We'd better begin operations over there on the left. There are fewer windows on that side. We can batter down the door. No, there is a high window above the door and they could shoot down upon us. That won't do. We'll take the left side. See, there are but two windows, both close together near the end. Look out, boys. Keep behind the trees. I wonder how solid those logs are. When was that church built, Captain Batts?"

"Don't remember the exact time, but not so very long ago. I recollect that there was talk of a probable extension, the time that new revivalist was having the house built, and that must account for the few windows toward this end on the left. They've got a first-rate place to shoot from, but what astonishes me is that Mayo should want to make a stand when he must know that we'll get him sooner or later."

"That's easily explained," said the scout who had dashed upon the public square. "They are looking for a large body of reinforcements from the south, and Mayo knows what to expect if he should run, panic-stricken, into them. His only hope was in making a stand."

"Where is Perdue?" the Major asked, looking about, from one tree to another.

"He fell back yonder in the field," old Gid answered. "I ran to him, but he must have been dead by the time he hit the ground."

The Major said nothing. He stood leaning against a tree looking toward Jim and four other men coming with the heavy door.

"And old Billy," said Gid, "is—"

The Major turned about. "Well," he broke in.

"You know," said Gid, "we used to say that he always had a blot of ink on his head. But now he's lying back yonder with a spot of blood where the ink was."

The Major called to Jim: "Put it down there." And then speaking to Gid he added: "That scoundrel must pay for this. Don't shoot him—don't even break his legs—I want to see them dangle in front of the court-house door."

With a chisel and a hammer the giant worked, on his knees, and it was almost like cutting through solid iron. The echo of his heavy blows rumbled afar off throughout the timber-land.

The detail of men came with the log, the body of a cypress tree, one end smoothly rounded. Jim took his measurements and proceeded with his work. Once he had to drag the door to a better-sheltered spot. Bullets from the church were pecking up the dirt about him. Three times the piece of timber was tried, to find that the hole in the door was not quite large enough, but at last it went through and the giant smiled at the neatness of the work. And now the ram was ready. The firing from the church had fallen and all was silent.

"It will take about eight men, four on a side—all strong young fellows," said Taylor. "You old men stand back. Major, order Captain Batts to let go the log."

"Captain Batts, turn loose," the Major commanded. "You are too old for such work."

With a sigh old Gid stepped back, and sadly he looked upon the young men as they took their places. "Yes, I'm getting old, John, but you needn't keep telling me of it."

"Sir, didn't I tell you not to call me John?"

"Yes, but I thought you'd forgotten it."

Taylor and the Englishman were side by side, the log between them. Auger holes had been bored in the shaft and strong oak pins had been driven in to serve for handles.

"Remember to keep a tight grip on your handle," said Jim.

"I warrant that," the Briton replied. "Are we all ready? Really quite a lark, you know."

A stable had stood at the left boundary of the field, and one wall, cut down, was now a part of the fence. Circling about to avoid the undergrowth and at the same time to keep out of Mayo's range, the men with the ram came up behind the old wall; and here they were halted to wait until the Major properly placed his marksmen. He made the circuit of the field, and coming back, announced that all was ready. A score of shot-guns were trained upon the two windows that looked out upon the space between the stable wall and the church. Over the wall the door was lifted, and the shot-guns roared, for the negroes had opened fire from the windows, but necessary caution marred the effect of their aim. Without a mishap the ram was lowered into the field. And now forward it went, slowly at first, but faster and faster, the men on a run, the lower edge of the door sweeping the old cotton stalks. Faster, with a yell, and the men about the field stood ready to charge. Shot-guns blazed from the windows, and shot like sharp sleet rattled off the heavy nail-heads in the door. Faster, and with a stunning *bim* the ram was driven against the house. But the logs lay firm. Back again, thirty feet, another run and a ram, but the logs were firm. From the windows, almost directly in front, the buck-shot poured, and glancing about, plucked up the dirt like raindrops in a dusty road. Once more, back still further, and again they drove with head-long force. The house shook, the roof trembled, but the logs were sound and stubbornly lay in place. Back again, but this time not to stop. "To the fence," Jim ordered. A shout came from the church. The Major stamped the ground. "Keep your places and wait for me," said Jim to his men. He leaped the stable wall. "Here, young fellow," he called, "run over to that store-house and bring a can of coal-oil. I was a fool not to think of this before. Why, even if we were to batter down the house they would kill us before our men could get there. Where is that axe?"

He seized the axe and began to split a dry pine log. Every one understood his plan; no one spoke. He split his kindling fine, whittled off shavings with his knife, and gathering up his faggots waited for the oil. The young fellow returned, running. Jim snatched the can and sprang over the fence. The Englishman smiled when he took his place. "Really you have quite an odd fancy, you know," he said.

"Once more and easy," Jim commanded. "And may the Lord have mercy on them. But it has to be done."

Onward they went, leaning inward, treading slowly, and shot was sleeted at them from the windows. But there was no quickening step as the house was neared—it was a dead march. At a corner of the church they halted, and Jim, putting down his oil can, close to the wall, piled his faggots about it, and then, striking a match, set fire to the shavings.

"Back!" he commanded.

They reached the stable wall and stood there. The guns were silent. Eagerly every one was gazing. Was the fire dying down? One long minute, and then a dull explosion. A column of flame shot high into the air, a rain of fire spattered down upon the church, and the roof was ablaze. The white men, ready with their guns, heard a trampling and the smothered cries of horror; and then the church door flew open and out poured Mayo and his men. Three times they charged an opening in the line about the fence, but unseen foes sprang up and mowed them down. But at the last, fighting, desperate, yelling, they broke out of the slaughter-pen and once more were in the woods. And now it was not even a chase. It was a still-hunt.

CHAPTER XXVI

CONCLUSION

Late in the afternoon, the news of the rout and the slaughter was received at the Cranceford home. All day Wash Sanders and his men had been sitting about, speculating, with but one stir of excitement, the boom of Mayo's cannon. But this soon died away and they sat about, swapping lies that were white with the mildew of time. But when news came they sprang astir for now they knew that each man must look after his own home, to protect it from fire. Some of them offered to remain, but Mrs. Cranceford dismissed them, assuring them that her house, being so public, was in no danger. So she was left, not alone, but with a score of women and children.

Afar off the guns could be heard, not in volleys, but the slow and fatal firing of men taking aim. The sun was nearly down when a man climbed over the fence and cautiously walked toward the house. In his hand he held a pine torch. Mrs. Cranceford grabbed a gun and ran out upon the porch.

"What are you doing there?" she demanded.

Larnage, the Frenchman, looked up at her and politely bowed.

"What are you doing there?" she repeated.

"Ah, is it possible that Madam does not suspect?" he replied, slowly turning his fire-brand, looking at the blaze as it licked the stewing turpentine.

"Yes, I do suspect, you villain, and if you don't throw down that torch this instant I'll blow your head off."

She brought the gun to her shoulder. He saw her close one eye, taking aim, and he stepped back and let his torch fall to the ground. "It shall be as Madam wishes," he said.

"Now you get out of this yard."

"Madam has but to command."

He passed through the gate and turned down the road; and upon him she kept a steady eye. She saw him leave the road and go into the woods.

Not far away was a potato-house, built over a cellar. To this frail structure he set fire. The dry timbers soon fell into the pit, and he stood there as if to warm himself. Night was his time for real work and he would wait. The sun was almost down. He turned away, and looking along the road that wound through the woods, he saw old Gideon coming. Quickly he hastened to the road-side and stood behind a tree, with a knife in his hand. Gid came slowly along. And just as he came abreast of the tree, his pop-eyes saw the fellow. He threw up his arm and caught the knife on the barrel of his gun; then leaping, with the gun clubbed, he struck at the Frenchman, but the fellow was too quick for him. "Oh, if I only had a cartridge!" the old man said with a groan, running after him. "I'd rather have a load of shot right now than a mortgage on Jerusalem. But I'll follow you—I'll get you."

Larnage was running, looking back, expecting to be shot; and stubbing his toe he fell—head-long into the potato-cellar, into the pit of red-hot coals. Ashes and a black smoke arose, and with frightful cries he scrambled out, and with his charred clothes falling off him, he ran to the bayou and plunged headforemost into the water. Gid saw him sink and rise; saw him sink again; and long he waited, but the man did not rise again.

* * * * *

Down along the bayou where negro cabins were thickly set, fires were springing up; and there, running from place to place, following white men who bore torches, was Father Brennon.

"Don't burn this house!" he cried. "It belongs to the church."

"Damn the church!" a man replied.

"But this house belongs to an innocent man—he would not seek to kill the whites—he's gone to the hills."

"I reckon you are right," said the man, and onward he ran, waving his torch, the priest keeping close behind him.

* * * * *

From the woods the men were coming, and as Gid drew near to the Cranceford house he saw Jim Taylor passing through the gate; and a few moments later, turning a corner of the porch, he found the giant standing there with his arm about—Louise.

"Ho, the young rabbit!" the old man cried.

"Frog," she laughed, running forward and giving him both her hands.

"Why, how did you get here?" he asked.

"I heard that the militia had been ordered home and I got here as soon as I could. I have been home about two hours and mother and I—but where is father?"

"Hasn't he come yet? Why, I thought he was here. We've all been scattered since the last stand."

"I will go and look for him," said the giant, taking up his gun from against the wall.

"I'm going with you," Louise declared. "Go on in the house, Uncle Gideon, and don't tell mother where I'm gone. Now, you needn't say a word—I'm going."

Down the road they went, and out into the woods. Far away they saw the cabins blazing, on the banks of the bayou, and occasionally a gun was heard, a dull bark, deep in the woods.

"You'd better go back," said Jim.

"No, I'm going with you. Oh, but this must have been an awful day—but let us not talk about it now." And after a time she said: "And you didn't suspect that I was doing newspaper work. They tell me that I did it well, too."

"I read a story in a newspaper that reminded me of you," he said. "It was called 'The Wing of a Bird.' It was beautiful."

"I didn't think so," she replied.

"Probably you didn't read it carefully," said he.

"I didn't read it carefully enough before I handed it in, I'm afraid," she replied.

"Oh, and did you write it?" He looked down at her and she nodded her head. "Yes, and I find that I do better with stories than at anything else," she said. "I have three accepted in the North and I have a book under way. That was the trouble with me, Jim; I wanted to write and I didn't know what ailed me, I was a crank."

"You are an angel."

He was leading her by the hand, and she looked up at him, but said nothing.

Just in front of them they saw the dying glow of a cabin in coals. A long clump of bushes hid the spot from view. They passed the bushes, looking to the left, and suddenly the girl screamed. Not more than twenty yards away stood the Major, with his back against a tree—gripping the bent barrel of a gun; and ten feet from him stood Mayo, slowly raising a pistol. She screamed and snatched the giant's gun and fired it. Mayo wheeled about, dropped his pistol, clutched his bare arm, and with the blood spouting up between his fingers he turned to flee. Two white men sprang out in from of him, and the Major shouted: "Don't kill him—he is to be hanged on the public square. I was trying to take him alive—and had to knock down two of his men. Tie him."

He held out his arms to Louise, and with her head on his breast and with mischief in her eyes, she looked up and said: "I have more than a daughter's claim on you. I have the claim of gallantry and upon this I base my plea."

He rebuked her with a hug and a kiss, saying not a word; but big Jim, standing there, turned about, laughing.

"What are you snorting at, Goliath? Has a David at last sunk a joke into your head? Come, let us go to the house."

"Father," said Louise, "I am going to show you how much I love you. And oh, how I longed to rest in your arms the time you held them out to me, in that desolate hall, the night of death; but I knew that if I yielded I would go back to the nest with my wings untried. I had to go away. I will tell you all about it, and I know that you will not be ashamed of me."

Silently they took their way homeward, choosing a shorter route; and coming upon an oozy place in the woods, Jim said to Louise: "I'm going to carry you in my arms." He did not wait for her to protest, but gathered her in his arms, and her head lay upon his shoulder.

"Do you want my love to build a mansion for your heart?" he whispered.

She put her arm about his neck.

They came out into the hard road, and still he carried her, with her arms tight about his neck. The Major looked on with a sad smile, for the sights of the day were still red before his eyes. But banteringly, he said: "First time I ever saw this hard road so muddy."

Louise laughed, whispered to Jim and he eased her to the ground.

"Why, they've burnt Wash Sanders' house!" the Major cried. "See, over there?"

They came opposite the place where the house had stood, and the Major suddenly drawing back, said to Jim: "Lead her around that way. She mustn't see this and she mustn't ask what it is."

Jim led her away, and the Major looked at Wash Sanders. Across a low rail fence his body lay, his hands drooping to the ground, and in front of him lay a gun that had fallen from his grasp; and a short distance away the Major found a mulatto, lying dead beside the road.

At the Major's house the women were preparing supper. The hungry men, some of them bleeding, had assembled in the yard. Darkness had fallen.

"Father," said Tom, coming forward, leading Sallie Pruitt by the hand, "mother says that this girl shall live with us."

"Yes," said the old man, putting his hands on Sallie's cheeks and kissing her. "Yes, my dear, you shall live with us." And turning to Low, he said: "You are a brave man. My hand, sir." And Low, grasping the old man's hand, replied: "I am an Englishman, and my father is a gentleman."

"Gid," said the Major, "my name is John, God bless you."

Down the road arose sharp words of command, and the burning top of a tall pine snag threw its light upon bayonets in the highway. The soldiers were come.

"I wonder what is to be the end of this day's beginning," said the Englishman.

"God only knows," the Major replied.

Friedrich Kerst
Friedrich Nietzsche
Fyodor Dostoyevsky
G.A. Henty
G.K. Chesterton
Gabrielle E. Jackson
Garrett P. Serviss
Gaston Leroux
George A. Warren
George Ade
Geroge Bernard Shaw
George Cary Eggleston
George Durston
George Ebers
George Eliot
George Gissing
George MacDonald
George Meredith
George Orwell
George Sylvester Viereck
George Tucker
George W. Cable
George Wharton James
Gertrude Atherton
Gordon Casserly
Grace E. King
Grace Gallatin
Grace Greenwood
Grant Allen
Guillermo A. Sherwell
Gulielma Zollinger
Gustav Flaubert
H. A. Cody
H. B. Irving
H.C. Bailey
H. G. Wells
H. H. Munro
H. Irving Hancock
H. R. Naylor
H. Rider Haggard
H. W. C. Davis
Haldeman Julius
Hall Caine
Hamilton Wright Mabie
Hans Christian Andersen
Harold Avery
Harold McGrath
Harriet Beecher Stowe
Harry Castlemon
Harry Coghill
Harry Houidini
Hayden Carruth
Helent Hunt Jackson
Helen Nicolay
Hendrik Conscience
Hendy David Thoreau
Henri Barbusse
Henrik Ibsen
Henry Adams
Henry Ford
Henry Frost
Henry James
Henry Jones Ford
Henry Seton Merriman
Henry W Longfellow
Herbert A. Giles
Herbert Carter
Herbert N. Casson
Herman Hesse
Hildegard G. Frey
Homer
Honore De Balzac
Horace B. Day
Horace Walpole
Horatio Alger Jr.
Howard Pyle
Howard R. Garis
Hugh Lofting
Hugh Walpole
Humphry Ward
Ian Maclaren
Inez Haynes Gillmore
Irving Bacheller
Isabel Cecilia Williams
Isabel Hornibrook
Israel Abrahams
Ivan Turgenev
J.G.Austin
J. Henri Fabre
J. M. Barrie
J. M. Walsh
J. Macdonald Oxley
J. R. Miller
J. S. Fletcher
J. S. Knowles
J. Storer Clouston
J. W. Duffield
Jack London
Jacob Abbott
James Allen
James Andrews
James Baldwin
James Branch Cabell
James DeMille
James Joyce
James Lane Allen
James Lane Allen
James Oliver Curwood
James Oppenheim
James Otis
James R. Driscoll
Jane Abbott
Jane Austen
Jane L. Stewart
Janet Aldridge
Jens Peter Jacobsen
Jerome K. Jerome
Jessie Graham Flower
John Buchan
John Burroughs
John Cournos
John F. Kennedy
John Gay
John Glasworthy
John Habberton
John Joy Bell
John Kendrick Bangs
John Milton
John Philip Sousa
John Taintor Foote
Jonas Lauritz Idemil Lie
Jonathan Swift
Joseph A. Altsheler
Joseph Carey
Joseph Conrad
Joseph E. Badger Jr
Joseph Hergesheimer
Joseph Jacobs
Jules Vernes
Julian Hawthrone
Julie A Lippmann
Justin Huntly McCarthy
Kakuzo Okakura
Karle Wilson Baker
Kate Chopin
Kenneth Grahame
Kenneth McGaffey
Kate Langley Bosher
Kate Langley Bosher
Katherine Cecil Thurston
Katherine Stokes
L. A. Abbot
L. T. Meade

L. Frank Baum
Latta Griswold
Laura Dent Crane
Laura Lee Hope
Laurence Housman
Lawrence Beasley
Leo Tolstoy
Leonid Andreyev
Lewis Carroll
Lewis Sperry Chafer
Lilian Bell
Lloyd Osbourne
Louis Hughes
Louis Joseph Vance
Louis Tracy
Louisa May Alcott
Lucy Fitch Perkins
Lucy Maud Montgomery
Luther Benson
Lydia Miller Middleton
Lyndon Orr
M. Corvus
M. H. Adams
Margaret E. Sangster
Margret Howth
Margaret Vandercook
Margaret W. Hungerford
Margret Penrose
Maria Edgeworth
Maria Thompson Daviess
Mariano Azuela
Marion Polk Angellotti
Mark Overton
Mark Twain
Mary Austin
Mary Catherine Crowley
Mary Cole
Mary Hastings Bradley
Mary Roberts Rinehart
Mary Rowlandson
M. Wollstonecraft Shelley
Maud Lindsay
Max Beerbohm
Myra Kelly
Nathaniel Hawthrone
Nicolo Machiavelli
O. F. Walton
Oscar Wilde
Owen Johnson
P.G. Wodehouse
Paul and Mabel Thorne
Paul G. Tomlinson
Paul Severing
Percy Brebner
Percy Keese Fitzhugh
Peter B. Kyne
Plato
Quincy Allen
R. Derby Holmes
R. L. Stevenson
R. S. Ball
Rabindranath Tagore
Rahul Alvares
Ralph Bonehill
Ralph Henry Barbour
Ralph Victor
Ralph Waldo Emmerson
Rene Descartes
Ray Cummings
Rex Beach
Rex E. Beach
Richard Harding Davis
Richard Jefferies
Richard Le Gallienne
Robert Barr
Robert Frost
Robert Gordon Anderson
Robert L. Drake
Robert Lansing
Robert Lynd
Robert Michael Ballantyne
Robert W. Chambers
Rosa Nouchette Carey
Rudyard Kipling
Saint Augustine
Samuel B. Allison
Samuel Hopkins Adams
Sarah Bernhardt
Sarah C. Hallowell
Selma Lagerlof
Sherwood Anderson
Sigmund Freud
Standish O'Grady
Stanley Weyman
Stella Benson
Stella M. Francis
Stephen Crane
Stewart Edward White
Stijn Streuvels
Swami Abhedananda
Swami Parmananda
T. S. Ackland
T. S. Arthur
The Princess Der Ling
Thomas A. Janvier
Thomas A Kempis
Thomas Anderton
Thomas Bailey Aldrich
Thomas Bulfinch
Thomas De Quincey
Thomas Dixon
Thomas H. Huxley
Thomas Hardy
Thomas More
Thornton W. Burgess
U. S. Grant
Upton Sinclair
Valentine Williams
Various Authors
Vaughan Kester
Victor Appleton
Victor G. Durham
Victoria Cross
Virginia Woolf
Wadsworth Camp
Walter Camp
Walter Scott
Washington Irving
Wilbur Lawton
Wilkie Collins
Willa Cather
Willard F. Baker
William Dean Howells
William le Queux
W. Makepeace Thackeray
William W. Walter
William Shakespeare
Winston Churchill
Yei Theodora Ozaki
Yogi Ramacharaka
Young E. Allison
Zane Grey

www.ingramcontent.com/pod-product-compliance
Lightning Source LLC
Chambersburg PA
CBHW020552310726
48979CB00008B/1192/J
9781421894577